BEFORE THE FALL

CAPTIVE HEARTS
BOOK FOUR

ABBI COOK

BEFORE THE FALL

I wasn't supposed to fall for Tia. She should have been no one to me.

She turned out to be the only soul I truly care about in this world. She knew what I was, and still she loved me. But every minute we spent together meant she wasn't safe because of the life I lead. I knew I had to let her go.

So I ignored my heart and walked away.

Now I find out what I did was all for nothing. She's marked for death by the head of my family.

Loyalty dictates I stand by as he kills her. Love demands I protect her with all I have. I'm nothing but a killer without her, but who am I without my family?

Published in the United States

ISBN: 979-8-9903606-1-7

CHAPTER ONE

axon

My eyes slowly open and the agony of the world's worst headache hits me like a freight train. Looking around, I wonder where the hell I am. Pink and green flowers on the sheets. Those billowy white curtains on the windows. This is definitely not my place.

I sit up and tilt my head left and then right to crack my neck. The sun streaming through the windows makes me squint, and I look away as my headache threatens to split my skull open.

My mouth doesn't possess an ounce of liquid, but I try to muster some by licking my lips with little success. Headache and cotton mouth. Now I remember. I'm hungover after a night of heavy drinking.

That explains where I am too. Ryker's place. This room screams Kaia's been here. She loves flowers and makes sure they're everywhere.

Pinching the bridge of my nose, I try to stave off my headache that's getting worse by the second. I would kill for a glass of water right now. Something to make this throbbing in my head disappear would be great too.

I throw the covers off me and swing my legs off the bed. So far, so good. When my feet hit the hardwood floor, the coolness feels incredible. But when I try to stand up, it's a no go. My equilibrium is all fucked up, and I collapse back on the bed.

A knock on the door interrupts the mess I am this morning, and a second later, Kaia walks into the room. "Good morning, Jaxon! Oh my!"

Unsure what's upset her, I look over at her and smile as she spins around to stand with her back to me. "If you have water and a handful of Advil, you'll be an angel sent from heaven. Any chance you have either of those things?"

Still not facing me, she waves her hand in my direction and says, "Can you throw the covers back over you? I think you must have forgotten you went to sleep with nothing on."

I glance down my body and chuckle. Grabbing the

sheet and blanket, I cover up a raging morning hard on. "Sorry about that," I groan. "I didn't even know where I was when I woke up, if that makes it any better."

Kaia cautiously turns around and smiles at me. "It's okay. I just felt like I was violating some unwritten rule seeing you like that. Do you feel sick this morning? Is that why you want the Advil?"

"Hungover," I answer as she walks over to the window and throws open the curtains. Jesus, that's bright.

Covering my eyes, I ask, "Do you think you could close those? The sun is killing me this morning."

"Oh, I'm so sorry. I wasn't thinking. I thought some fresh air would make you feel better."

I've slept at Ryker's before, and never once has Kaia come to see me first thing in the morning. Something must be up.

"Is everything okay?" I ask as I sit up again.

She tries to smile, but it never makes it up to her eyes. "Ryker wants to see you as soon as you can get down to his office. I'll grab you some water and Advil. I'll leave it on the dresser, okay?"

"How serious is it? Do I have time for a shower?" I ask as she starts to leave.

Kaia stops at the door and nods. "I think so. Get cleaned up and come down when you can."

She leaves me alone with my headache, dry mouth, and thoughts about what could have happened this morning. Everything was great last night. We drank all that German beer Kane loves, and Cason even joined us, a rarity now that Lily is pregnant with their second child. He usually likes to stay close to her, but we got him to come out and enjoy himself with the guys for the first time in months.

No doubt the issue has to do with Victor. It's always him ever since Ryker decided the time was coming to overthrow him as the leader of the family. He's waited while he got his ducks in a row, and now it's just a matter of striking when the time is right.

Maybe that's today.

If so, I'm ready for it. I lost the only woman I've ever loved because of that asshole. Nothing made me happier than being with Tia, but I couldn't keep putting her in danger as long as he was the head of the Varens family. I don't know if she can ever forgive me, but once Victor is gone, I'm going to damn well try my best to convince her to take me back.

I better get this day going because if today is the day we get rid of that fuck, I want to be in top form. A nice, hot shower should do the trick.

RYKER SITS BEHIND HIS DESK WITH CASON AND Kane in the chairs in front of him. Some other guy whose name I can't remember right now sits on the sofa talking to a guy I've never seen before. As I walk into the room, all eyes turn toward me.

"What's up? And a bigger question, why aren't the rest of you dealing with the world's worst hangover this morning?"

Cason laughs at me as he shakes his head. "You're such a fucking lightweight. Eat some aspirin and stop whining."

As I take a seat in a chair across the room from him, I mumble, "That seems harsh, motherfucker."

Ryker studies me for a long moment and then he shakes his head too. "You look like shit warmed over today, Jaxon. I'm not sure you're up for what we have to talk about this morning."

I wave off his worry. "I'm fine. Just a little headache, but your lovely wife gave me some Advil. Assuming they'll kick in soon, I'll be fit as a fiddle in a minute or two. What's going on? Why the powwow at this time of day on a Sunday?"

Suddenly, neither he nor Cason have anything to say. Odd. Granted, neither man is usually chatty, but this is supposed to be a meeting to discuss something, so what's up?

"Cat got your tongue?" I ask no one in particular.

The four men around me look at each other and then everyone turns their focus to Ryker. Since he's the one in charge, I do the same and wait for him to start talking.

When he still doesn't, I ask, "What's going on, Ryker? Did someone die?"

My question comes off sounding like a joke, but I

couldn't be more serious. If it's Victor who's dead, he'd be all kinds of happy, so I know that problem hasn't been magically solved. Then I start listing relatives of ours in my head, wondering which one isn't with us anymore.

"Dash over there has been working for Victor for the past few months. He's with us, though, and he's been keeping an eye out for any news we can use. This morning, he told me about a job he's been assigned concerning someone you know."

Okay, it's not that someone's dead but someone is going to be dead soon. But who could it be? I don't have friends since I'm a killer. I spend nearly all my time with these guys.

So who is this person I know who Victor's decided isn't long for this world?

After a few seconds, I shrug and try to make light of the situation. "I think you guys are mistaken. I don't have a social life to speak of for the past couple years, so I can't imagine who's managed to get on the wrong side of Victor."

That must be it. They think I know this person with the target on his back, but they're wrong.

Ryker's expression grows even darker than usual, and he blows the air out of his lungs like he hates what he has to say. I don't think I've ever seen my uncle concerned like this.

"Are you going to tell me, or are we all going to just sigh like a bunch of teenage girls? Who the fuck does Victor have his eye on, Ryker?" I finally ask, tired of hearing no answers to my questions.

"It's Tia's father, Jaxon."

Just hearing her name come out of his mouth makes my heart skip a beat. But he's got something wrong. Tia's father is a straight-laced guy, a perfectly upper middle class dad who would never get tangled up with the likes of Victor Varens.

I shake my head and smile. "Someone's got their wires crossed, guys. Tia's father stays on the right side of the law. Always. Trust me on this."

He frowns, and when I look around the room, everyone else looks as unhappy as he does. "Jaxon, it's no mistake. Tia's father got into some bad things a few years ago, and he began associating with a man named Rudolf Michner."

That name rolls around in my brain for a few moments, but I have nothing. I've never heard of that person.

"Even if that's true, what does that have to do with Victor? Has your brother suddenly decided to take on other bosses' problems?"

Ryker nods, which surprises me. That's not like Victor. He's always been a lone wolf to his core. He doesn't even like sharing power with his own brother.

"Michner and Victor worked together on a few deals. It seems as a partner, Michner wasn't too great because Victor had him killed. Now he's looking to get all he can out of the people who owed his old partner.

I don't know if he's made the connection between you and Tia and her father, but if he does, I'm worried she's in as much danger as her father is."

With every word, my blood runs cold. I walked away from Tia and all the happiness she brought me for this very goddamned reason. I never wanted her to suffer because of what I do for a living. I thought I made sure she'd be protected when I broke it off with her. Now I hear that I missed having an entire year of utter bliss with the woman I love and still she's not safe?

I turn to face Dash and ask, "What did Victor say? I want to hear every fucking word exactly as he said it."

He looks over at Ryker, but before he can say a word, I snap, "Don't look at him. Look at me, asshole. You heard Victor say the words, so I want to hear what he's planning."

The room feels like everyone has suddenly become frozen in place except for me. I jump up, ready to shake the hell out of this Dash guy to find out what I need to know, but Cason stops me before I can make a move.

"Calm down, Jaxon. We're not going to let anyone hurt Tia or her family. You know that."

I look at him and see a smile. "What the fuck is good about this that you're fucking grinning? The woman I love might be in danger, even though I've forced myself to live without her to make sure she didn't get sucked into my life and get hurt, and her father has a target on his goddamned back. None of that seems like it warrants a fucking smile, man."

He frowns like he wants to make sure I know he's on my side. "I was just trying to make you see it's going to be okay."

Ryker stands up and walks over to join us. "We won't let anything or anyone hurt her, Jaxon. Give Cason a break. He's trying to keep you calm so you don't go off half-cocked."

"Then how about I go off all cocked? I'm not feeling this get together and chat about shit vibe you all have this morning now that I know Tia might get hurt."

Turning to look at Cason, I push him away from me. "And fuck that calm shit you're giving me. I don't need to be calm. I need to make sure she's safe and handle things so she doesn't lose her father."

"That's exactly what we're going to help you do. Sit down so we can plan things out," Ryker says behind me.

Unsure I want to sit down when all I want to do is rush to where Tia is to protect her, I stand firm for a long moment before deciding that having my family's help is a good thing. As we all take our seats again, I have only one question.

"Tell me again why we haven't killed this motherfucker yet?"

Ryker smiles like I said something funny. "Strange

that you should ask that today since that's exactly what I've been thinking myself. My brother is out of control. I've waited in the hope that he would settle down, but I see now that isn't going to happen."

"So why the hell aren't we striking this morning? You've had Dash over there spying for you for months. What's the hold up?"

"Timing is important, Jaxon. I have everyone to consider, and until now, I haven't wanted to put a bullet in my own brother's head."

His answer doesn't jive with me. "Sentimental now? Is this what happens when a guy settles down?"

Rage fills my uncle's eyes, and he snaps, "There are parts of my life you don't get to comment on. Don't make the mistake again, or you'll find out what happens when you step over the line. We're family, but that will only take you so far. Ask my brother about that."

"The fact that I can still ask him anything fucking baffles me," I say, not giving a damn about Ryker's feelings on the matter at this moment. "If he was dead, Tia and her father wouldn't be in danger."

"About that. I don't know if you'll be able to save Tia's father. Tia we can protect, but if Victor sees any of us around him, that may tip our hand."

Most of the time, I appreciate Ryker's ability to calmly judge a situation and not let emotions get in the way. This isn't one of those times.

Sick of everything I've heard at this meeting, I

stand up, shaking my head. "Then I'll protect them. I can't let Tia lose her father because we're too chickenshit to move on Victor. You do what you have to, Ryker. I'm going to make sure she and her father stay alive."

Nobody tries to stop me as I march out of his office. Good. I don't want to have to fuck up anyone in my family today.

CHAPTER TWO

axon

I SEE THE ROAD SIGN FOR CHARLOTTE AND KNOW
I'm close to Tia. I may have thought I could protect
her by leaving, but for me, she's never truly been far
from my mind. I make this trip at least twice a month,
needing to see her, even if she can't see me.

She'd be furious if she knew. She'd glare at me and
call me a stalker. She wouldn't be wrong.

But it wouldn't matter what she said. I'd still be
happier than I've been since I left her to hear her say
even a single word to me.

A whole year is a long time to want and not be able
to have. To not be able to even touch her or smell the

soft scent of her perfume. To be without the one person you love more than anything else in the world.

It was my choice, though. I have no one to blame but myself for having to live without her. But even thinking about that last time I saw her makes my chest ache.

I watch as Tia washes the dishes, knowing what I plan to do tonight is going to be the hardest thing I've ever done. All day I've dreaded it, even as I can't deny it's the only way she'll be safe. I've been lying to myself for too long. I wanted to believe what we are could be separate from my work for my family, but that's just a dream that could never come true.

She deserves a life that doesn't involve the danger that comes from being with me.

"Do you want to go down to the lake?" she asks, tearing me out of my terrible thoughts about what I'm about to do.

Shaking my head, I grimace. "Not tonight."

Instead of showing disappointment, she merely shrugs and gives me a cute smile. "Okay. I just thought maybe you didn't want to stay in again."

Tia giggles before turning back to finish washing the dishes. I hate that what I'm about to say will make this the last time she's happy around me.

"When you're done there, I want to talk," I say quietly, still not sure I'll be able to do this, although I don't have a choice.

She looks back at me and nods. "Okay. I just have a fork and spoon to do, and then I'm all yours."

I give her a tiny smile that barely hides how miserable I

am right now. I'd give the world to not have to say these terrible words.

I don't take my eyes off her, needing to fill my mind with the memory of Tia happy. Even standing at the sink in a pair of gray yoga pants and an old UNC T-shirt with her blond hair up in a messy ponytail, she's the most beautiful woman I've ever seen.

How the hell am I going to say I never want to see her again?

I hear her shut off the faucet, and my chest tightens. As she dries her hands on that dish towel with the roosters on it, I suddenly can't remember how I wanted to start this conversation. Fuck. I had this whole thing plotted out in my mind as I was driving down here yesterday afternoon. I found the perfect way to say what I need to, and now I can't remember a goddamned word of it.

"You seem quiet tonight, Jaxon. Something on your mind?" she asks sweetly, far too nice for someone like me.

Smiling, even though happiness has no place inside me now, I nod. God, I can't bring myself to say anything right now.

"You said you wanted to talk. What's up?" she asks with a playful lilt in her voice that tells me she has no idea what's coming next.

I clear my throat, but it's like every word I need to say is stuck in there. This shouldn't be so hard. Tia deserves to be away from the kind of danger I bring to her life. I know this is for the best, but I'm not thinking with my head right now.

My heart's in charge, and it doesn't want me to let her go.

"I just felt like we need to talk," I say, barely able to utter even those syllables.

"Okay," she says with an adorable smile as she walks around the table to sit on my lap. "What's on your mind?"

Jesus, all I can think about is how much I love feeling her next to me. I don't think I can do this. I can't break up with her tonight. Maybe tomorrow when I'm leaving to head back to Pennsylvania. That would be a better time to do this.

I look into her beautiful eyes and see so much love in them. I don't deserve her or the sweetness she brings to my life. I'm a killer. That she forgave me for how we met and what I did back then only proves that she deserves better than me.

"Is something wrong, Jaxon? You look like you're going to be sick."

Even as I shake my head, I know I have to tell her.

I lift Tia off my lap and set her on her feet next to me before standing. I can't face her when I say this, so I focus my attention on that spot on the wall from that time when we were playing around and I knocked over her lamp by mistake. It left a dimple in the plaster I keep telling myself I'll fix the next time I come down to see her, but I never get around to it.

Now it will be a permanent feature of the wall. Or worse, the next guy she starts dating will fix it. Fuck, I hate the idea of her with anyone else.

If only there was another way.

"So I think I'm going to have to stop coming here," I mumble, hating how the words sound as they leave my mouth.

Beside me, Tia makes a noise that reminds me of how I sound every time I've been shot. It's the sound of utter agony.

"What? I don't...I don't understand." she says with so much hurt in her voice that a knot forms in the pit of my stomach.

I take a step toward the door and stop, still not looking at her as I continue. "I just think it's time."

Fuck, none of this is coming out like I want it to. I promised myself I wouldn't be a jackass when I told her, and that's exactly how I sound.

"Time for what? I don't know what you're talking about."

Finally, I turn to face her and see pure sadness in her expression. "It's been fun, hasn't it? We had some great times together. I just think it's time to say goodbye."

Tears fill her eyes as she shakes her head. "Why are you saying this? You're breaking up with me? Why? What happened, Jaxon?"

"Nothing happened. I just think it's time. This whole long distance thing was always going to be hard. Turns out it was harder than I thought it would be. It's okay. We made some good memories, right?"

My casual way of saying I don't want to see her anymore only makes things worse, and Tia begins to cry. It's breaking my heart to see her so sad and to know I'm the reason she feels like this. I want to take her into my arms and say I was only making a bad joke. She's kind. She'd accept that after slapping me across the face, which is something I deserve at this moment.

But I can't go back now. Every moment I'm with Tia puts her in danger. It's better to hurt her like this than to have her suffer far worse because of me.

Finally, the floodgates open, and tears stream down her face. She pushes against my chest, angry at me like she should be.

"Why are you talking about our time together like it meant nothing to you? Did it? Did it mean absolutely nothing to you all these months?" she sobs.

I shrug, knowing how fucking disrespectful that is right now. "It meant a lot to me. I just think it's time."

Her tear-filled eyes flash anger I've only seen a few times in Tia. "Time? You keep saying that! Why? Why is it time now?"

I'd hoped I wouldn't have to use the nuclear option, but she's not going to let me off the hook. Not that I blame her. It's not like I've given her any valid reason for not wanting to be with her anymore. What does a few hours driving to see her mean to me? I never minded the trip down here, so she knows that's a bullshit reason for wanting to break up.

So I swallow hard and say the hardest words I've ever uttered in my life.

"I've met someone else. She's closer, so we don't have to do the long distance relationship thing."

As each syllable leaves my mouth, Tia grows sadder and sadder until she collapses onto the chair. "You met someone else? How could you do this to us? I guess there was no us, though. Not if you could find someone new."

Fuck, I want to get the hell out of this place right now. I can't see her like this.

When I don't say anything, she jumps up from the chair and shakes her head as tears continue to stream down her cheeks. "I'll never forgive you, Jaxon. Whoever she is, I hope she makes you happier than I did."

That's not possible. I want to tell her that, but I can't. Keeping her safe is too important to turn back now.

"Thanks. I hope we can be friends," I say like some stereotypical dick just asking for someone to slap their face.

"Friends?" she repeats in disbelief. "I don't want to be friends with you. You've broken my heart, and now you think friends is something we can be? Go fuck yourself, Jaxon. Go to whoever this new girl is and never darken my doorstep again. I never want to see you again in my life!"

She storms away as my heart sinks, and when she slams her bedroom door, it's like she's put up a barrier I couldn't get through even if I tried. I want to, but if I go back on my plan now, she'll never be safe because I'll never be able to say goodbye to her again.

Feeling like someone's ripped open my chest and tore my heart out with their bare hands, I stand in Tia's kitchen and try to memorize how this place looks. I want to always remember how happy I was in this room.

How happy and selfish because I knew being with Tia could mean her life.

At least I've remedied that. Now she just hates me.

Memories of that night make me sick to my stomach, so I take a gulp from my water bottle to push the bile back down. I could drive this route in my sleep since I've done it so many times, even since I left her.

I've never missed anyone like I have since I told

Tia goodbye, but I thought it was for the best. Now I can't wait to see her again.

I park outside her apartment and think about how she gave up on her dreams of being a psychologist this year. Was that because of me? I don't know. All I do know is she's too smart to be working as some assistant to a bank president.

When I step out onto the sidewalk, it's like the past comes rushing back to me. I used to watch over her like this in the early days. I'd stand on the sidewalk across the street from her house and wait to see even a glimpse of her.

Staring up at her living room window, I wait for her to walk by as I realize I've missed her even more than I thought I did. She doesn't appear, so after ten minutes, I begin walking to her door. I'm more nervous than I've ever been in my life. I know what I should expect, but what if I see a man there with her?

Jealousy surges inside me, but I take a deep breath and knock on her door. My heart slams into my chest as I wait to see my first glimpse of her beautiful face in far too long.

The door opens, and there she is staring out at me with the same sweetness I've always loved in her eyes. She shakes her head as she backs away. She doesn't invite me in, but I walk inside anyway, thrilled to see her.

"What makes you think you're welcome here? Do

you always just walk into women's homes like you own them?" she snaps, her anger filling her voice.

I don't answer either of her questions. I know I'm not welcome in her world. Not after what I did. That doesn't matter, though.

"Why are you here?" she asks flatly, but I sense the emotion in her she's trying so hard to hide.

"I need to see you."

She frowns and shakes her head again. "Well, I don't want to see you."

I take a step toward her and smile. "Yes, you do. Trust me."

Tia's eyes open wide, and I see nothing kind or loving in them. "Trust you? Is that supposed to be a joke? Because I'm not laughing."

Another step brings me to right in front of her, and I stop. "No joke, Tia."

She stares up at me with such sadness in her eyes that my heart breaks. I'm dying to kiss her after so long, but when I lean in, Tia slaps me hard across the face.

"That's for breaking my heart. Now go back to your girlfriend before I do something worse."

I watch as she marches out of the room and can't deny I deserved that slap. I actually deserve so much more.

But what does she mean she's going to do something worse?

CHAPTER THREE

ia

MY HANDS SHAKE LIKE LEAVES IN A HURRICANE AS I try to pretend I'm strong and don't give a damn about seeing Jaxon again. Oh, God. All that therapy and the first time he's in front of me again I can't deny I'm a mess. I thought if I ever saw him again I'd be able to handle it.

How wrong I was. One look at him and it was like all the time apart meant nothing and I was back in my old apartment where he broke up with me.

Wait a second. That's right. I need to remember that detail. He broke up with me. He left me for another woman, so whatever he's doing here means nothing.

I can't deal with him right now. How dare he come to my apartment like nothing ever happened? Like he didn't shatter my heart when he left me.

Like he has any right to just march into my home.

Feeling myself slip into a place I swore I wouldn't visit ever again, I hurry to my room and lock the door behind me. I need to not see him. If I don't see him when he talks to me, I'll be able to hold strong and not crumble to pieces.

"Tia, come out here. I need to talk to you."

Why is he acting like he has any right to be standing in my living room right now ordering me to do what he wants? Who the hell does he think he is?

"Go away! I don't want to see you. You aren't welcome here, Jaxon!"

Ah, there's that fire my therapist told me to never let go of. I wasn't sure it still existed, especially when I saw him at my door and all I wanted to do was throw my arms around him. As Dr. Atkins always tells me, it's okay to care about someone. That doesn't mean they get to be a part of my life.

Now if I can just remember that when Jaxon refuses to leave.

I hear his footsteps as he walks down the hall toward my room. They stop just outside my door, and then a second later, he tries to turn the handle.

He really does think he has some right to be here. He needs to get the hint he's mistaken.

"Tia, please come out. I need to talk to you. It's important."

The hint of sadness in his voice makes my willpower falter ever so slightly, but then I remember the reason he said he needed to leave me. "Just go. I want you to leave me be."

"I can't."

My stomach twists into a tight knot when I hear that. He said that the night he came to see me after that terrible week I spent out at his house. He said he couldn't get me out of his mind then. Now what's his reason why he has to come here and bother me?

"Why? What makes it impossible for you to leave my house, where incidentally, you aren't welcome, Jaxon? Did your girlfriend leave you?"

I don't care that my voice sounds like I'm gloating. I hope she did leave him. Maybe he finally understands what it felt like when he broke up with me.

"No."

"Then go back to her and leave me alone," I say through the door, not caring that I may be hurting his feelings.

He ripped my heart out when he left me. Turnabout's fair play.

"Let me in, Tia."

The way he always sounds like he's in the right and I must listen to him still comes through loud and clear in every word he says. The difference now is I'm not the same girl he left behind in a pool of her own tears.

That Tia is long gone.

"No. I spent all those months trying to get over you. I finally did, so I won't let you do this to me again."

He's quiet after my defiant little speech, and I begin to wonder if he's thinking about leaving. He should. It would be better for both of us.

I listen for the sound of his footsteps to let me know he's walking away, but I hear nothing. That means I'm still in danger of letting him back in. I have to remember that.

"Do what to you again?" he asks, as if he doesn't know his own crimes when it comes to me.

As much as I want to stay angry, that question makes my chest hurt. My answer comes out in quiet voice as I try not to cry.

"Break my heart."

He sighs against the door before saying, "I never wanted to do that."

"Well, you did," I say as I will those damn tears of mine to go the hell away. "Just go. Let me live my life. I was finally happy. After months of feeling like I'd never smile again, I'm okay now. If you ever cared for me, you'll leave and never come back, Jaxon."

"Tia, I'm here because I care for you. You have to let me in."

I notice he doesn't use the past tense and instead

says care, like it's something he still feels. No! I can't let myself get sucked into dissecting his words and wondering what they mean. He told me loud and clear that he didn't want to see me anymore that night in my old apartment. Nothing's changed.

He's still the same bad man he always was.

"Go away, Jaxon. I moved on. I found someone who cares about me. I hope you can find the same."

Every word of that is a lie. I've never been able to move on. Oh, I thought I did, but as soon as I saw him standing in front of me tonight, that became a lie I'd told myself during all those months alone. None of the men I've dated could make me forget Jaxon. Even the thought of him happy with someone makes my heart hurt to this moment.

"Who? Who is he?" he asks, and I hear genuine jealousy in his voice.

Why?

Even more importantly, who does he think he is asking me that?

I throw the door open and stare at him in disbelief. "I can't believe you have the nerve to ask me that."

He smiles, even though my question wasn't anything nice or funny. "I just said that hoping you'd get angry enough to open the door. I know I have no right to even be here."

I hate that he knew just asking me that question would work. He's right about one thing, though. He has no right being here or expecting me to be kind to him after what he did.

As he looks into my eyes, he says, "I missed you, Tia. Not a day has gone by that I didn't think of you."

So now he misses me? Where was he all those nights I lay in bed crying?

I push past him to walk out to the living room. "So you were a terrible boyfriend to another woman. How nice."

Behind me, he says in a low voice, "There was no girlfriend, Tia."

Spinning around to face him, I snap, "Don't insult my intelligence. I remember you saying there was someone else."

His face is expressionless when he answers, "I lied."

"What? Why?" I ask, my head swimming with questions.

When he doesn't answer, I ask, "Why would you tell me that? You broke my heart. I wanted to die when you dumped me. Now you stand here telling me you lied? Why? Did you just want to be away from me?"

Still, he refuses to answer me, so I pound on his chest, needing to make him hurt like I hurt right now. Like I hurt when he left me.

"How could you do that to me? I loved you, Jaxon."

He grabs my wrists to stop me from hitting him, so

I turn my back to him. "Don't. You deserve whatever I do to you," I sob, unable to hold back my tears any longer.

Jaxon rests his chin on my shoulder and quietly says, "I loved you. I still do. I've never stopped, Tia."

I can't listen to this.

Turning in his hold, I try to yank my arms from him but he won't let go. "Well, I have."

"No, you haven't. A love like the kind we have doesn't go away."

"Maybe not for you, but I got over it," I lie, but it's no use.

He has no idea how much I wish I could have moved on. It's all I wanted for months, but it never happened.

"I don't believe you. You couldn't get over me any more than I could get over you."

I shake my head, desperate to not let him see how much he affects me. "I don't care if you believe me! I want you to leave. Now!"

He pulls me to him and kisses me, and in a flash, it's like he never left. Like always, his kiss takes my breath away. I've missed him so much, and I can't fight that truth anymore.

When I begin to cry harder, he holds me tightly to him and whispers against the top of my head, "I'm sorry, Tia. I left because I wanted to keep you safe."

I don't understand and look up at him, confused.

"You broke my heart, Jaxon. Is that the kind of safety you meant?"

He dries my tears by gently dragging the pad of his thumb across the tops of my cheeks. "I stayed away, even though it killed me not to be near you."

"Every night for months, I cried myself to sleep. I didn't want to miss you, but I couldn't help it."

Leaning down, he presses a kiss to my forehead and whispers, "I'm sorry. Forgive me."

I want to say I can't forgive him. I can't lie, though. I've never stopped loving him.

CHAPTER FOUR

ia

EVERY INCH OF MY BODY CRAVES HIS TOUCH, JUST like it's always been. There's just something about Jaxon that never fails to make me forget everything.

How angry I am at him. How much on paper we don't work. How we're as different as night and day.

None of it matters when he's near me.

"So there was never another woman? Do you know how much it hurt thinking you met someone else and didn't care about me anymore?"

He nods, frowning as he acknowledges what he did. "I was trying to do something good, for once, Tia. I never wanted to leave you, but things just got too dangerous and I wanted to protect you. That's the God's honest truth."

I want to believe him. I truly do. Nobody in the world has ever made me happier than Jaxon, but if he was trying to keep me safe, why is he here today?"

"Why did you come back? Is it that I'm not in danger anymore? By the way, as much as I love the knight in shining armor thing you were doing, I think it would have been much better if you had given me some clue as to what I should have been worried about. It's not like you were here watching me day and night to make sure I was safe."

Jaxon sighs and sits down on the couch. "I didn't want to upset you."

"Be honest. You didn't want me to be able to say that once again your job is a problem. At least admit that so we can be truthful with one another now."

He gives me a smile and pats the cushion next to him. "Fair enough. I know how you feel about my job. That wasn't it, though. I made sure you were safe by not being around you. If I was with you, then you could be a target to hurt me. But I did check on you."

I sit down next to him and shake my head. "So you got to see me, but I didn't get that little bonus."

"You can't think seeing you without ever being able to touch you or even just be next to you was any kind of bonus. It was killing me to be able to know what's going on in your life without being near you."

As hard as it is, I do believe him. I lean back on the

couch and blow the air out of my lungs as I try to wrap my brain around all that's happened tonight.

"So you never had another girlfriend, and I was in danger. Good to know."

He turns to face me. "And I missed you. Don't forget that part because it's important," he says with a sexy smile that makes my stomach do a flip.

"I missed you too," I admit, not afraid to let him know the truth about how I felt these past twelve months. "But if I was in danger and you were keeping me safe, does this visit tonight mean I'm out of danger?"

Jaxon shakes his head as sadness fills his expression. "I wish that was the case, but no. I'm here tonight because you're in even more danger now than last year."

"So the year we spent apart was for nothing?" I ask on the verge of tears at hearing that all the misery I went through could have been avoided.

Gently, he sets his hands on my shoulders and pulls me to him. "No, it was necessary because I was afraid you'd be hurt. The situation has changed, and not for the better, so now the danger is even worse. But don't worry. I promise I won't let anyone hurt you or anyone you love."

His heart races against my cheek as his soft words filter through my brain. He won't let anyone I love get hurt?

Leaning back, I look into his eyes. "What does that

mean, no one I love? Is someone I'm close to in danger?"

He answers with a nod as he returns to frowning. "Yeah. Your father."

I shake my head in disbelief. That's not possible. My father is one of the kindest people I know. No one would want to hurt him.

"No. I don't believe that. Why would he be in danger?"

Jaxon sighs like he doesn't want to tell me the truth. "I promise I won't let anyone hurt him, Tia. I swear."

"You still haven't explained why he'd be in danger. You have to be mistaken. My father is a sweet man who goes to work every day, comes home and helps my mother with dinner, and even washes the dishes sometimes. That kind of man doesn't run into the kind of people who could put him in danger."

When Jaxon doesn't say anything, I jump up from the couch shaking my head. "None of this is true, is it? You just made this up so you could explain away leaving me for a year. Just go! Get out of my life and leave me alone!"

I run to my room and slam the door, but before I can lock it and him out, he walks in like he owns the place. "Tia, I didn't make anything up. There was no other woman. I've never stopped loving you. I left because I thought that was the best way to keep you safe, but unfortunately, that isn't the way it worked out. Your father got involved with some guy my uncle was partners with. He owed him some money. My uncle killed the guy, but now he plans to handle the people he was working with, like your father. I don't know much more right now, but I drove down here to see you because I was worried. I swear to you all I've said tonight is the truth."

None of this makes sense. My father wouldn't associate with anyone who could put him in danger. What on earth is Jaxon talking about?

"I can't believe this. What is the man's name? What did my father do with him?"

Jaxon shakes his head. "I don't know."

"Well, find out because if you don't, I won't believe you."

Folding my arms across my chest, I sit down hard on the bed. "If you can't answer those questions, then you should just go."

He begins to pace back and forth from one side of my bedroom to the other shaking his head. I've seen him like this before. Jaxon is the kind of man who expects people to believe him when he tells them something, and the fact that I've pretty much just said I don't buy any of this bothers him.

Good. It should. No one should barge into someone's life like he's come into mine tonight and lay all this madness on them. It's not right.

Suddenly, he stops in front of where I'm sitting on the bed and stares down at me with a wildness in his eyes that frightens me. "Michner. Rudolf Michner. That was the guy's name. I don't know what your father was doing with him, but that's his name."

I reach over to my nightstand and grab my phone to call my father. "Fine. I'll ask my father about him, and if he admits to knowing him, then I'll believe you."

My father's phone rings a few times, and I get ready for it to go to voicemail, but then he answers like he always does, so sweet and happy to hear from me. "Tia, honey. I didn't expect to hear from you today. What's up?"

"Hi, Daddy. I need to ask you something, and I want you to be honest with me. Please, can you promise to do that?" I ask, my heart slamming into my chest because I'm so scared to hear his answer to my question.

"Sure, honey. What's on your mind?"

"Do you know anyone named Rudolf Michner?"

I expect him to answer immediately, but the phone falls silent. Why isn't he answering?

"Did you hear me?" I ask, hoping the phone call simply dropped or went out for a second there.

"Yes, sweetheart. I heard you. Where did you hear that name?" my father asks, avoiding answering my question.

"Please, Daddy. Just tell me yes or no. Do you know a man named Rudolf Michner?"

My hand shakes as I hold the phone to my ear and await his answer. Why isn't he simply answering me?

"Yes, I do. He's dead now, though, but I did know him. Why do you ask?" my father answers in a low voice.

"How did you know him?" I ask as I look up at Jaxon as he waits to hear what I'm hearing.

"It's a long story, honey. Maybe someday I'll tell you, but not now."

"Yes, now!" I say, practically sobbing. "I need to know. How did you know that man?"

Again, the phone falls silent, but I don't wonder if the call dropped this time. I know what's happening. I've seen this before when my parents fight. When my father's in the wrong, he hesitates to say what needs to be said.

Finally, he answers, "I had to borrow money off him. After what happened to you, I wanted to take you and your mother on that trip. Do you remember how much fun we had when we went to Spain for those two weeks? Well, I didn't have the money to pay for all of it, so I borrowed some. It's okay, though, because I paid it all back."

My heart sinks as I listen to his explanation. He needed that money because of me and what I was going through. He's in trouble because of me.

"Okay, Daddy," I say with so much sadness it practically drips off every word. "Thank you for being honest. I have to go now. I'll see you soon, okay?"

"Okay, Tia. Are you feeling sick or something? You don't sound right tonight."

"I'm fine. I'll talk to you later."

My heart feels like it's going to break after hearing the answer I dreaded. Setting my phone back on the nightstand, I lie back on the bed as I try not to cry.

"What did he say?" Jaxon asks, but I turn my back to him.

When I don't answer, he climbs onto the bed and wraps his arms around me. "It's going to be okay, Tia. I promise I'm going to take care of it."

Something about the way he says that makes me want to scream. I turn in his hold and stare into his dark eyes as rage fills me.

"My father had to borrow money to take my family on a trip. And do you know why he felt like he wanted to take my mother and me on a damn trip, Jaxon? Because I was a fucking mess after that week you kept me out at that house. My father is in trouble because of you, and now you say you're going to take care of it? Why don't you just leave me alone? Just go and let me and my family live in peace."

He stares at me in horror for a few moments but says nothing. Fine. I doubt he'd be able to say anything that I'd want to hear anyway.

Rolling over, I turn my back to him again and say in a low voice into the pillow, "Leave, Jaxon. You've done enough damage."

I don't know how long he stays with me, but at

some point, I feel the mattress dip and then he leaves without another word. Maybe it's unfair to blame everything on him. I don't know.

All I know is I thought I was getting over him, and now I'm a mess again after seeing him.

CHAPTER FIVE

axon

For two hours, I sit in my car in front of her house and wait to see her, but she never appears. She's right. This is all my fault. I tried to make it up to her after what I did when we met because I love her. I've never loved anyone like this. It nearly tore me apart to break up with her last year, another one of my great ideas that ended up hurting her.

This is different, though. If I don't do something, Tia and her parents are going to get hurt because of Victor.

Because of me.

I stare up at her windows wishing for nothing

more than a glimpse of Tia. She knows I'm out here. She knows me better than anyone else on earth, so of course, she knows.

That's why she's avoiding letting me see her. She's punishing me.

Not that I don't deserve it. I know I do, and still I need to stay here in case she appears.

So much of what we've been together has been sweeter than anything else I've encountered in my life. Tia brings out the best in me. No one else sees that side of me but her. It's like I can't help but be kinder when it comes to her. I kill for a living, but with Tia, all I want to do is protect and love her and everything and everyone she cares about.

She teases out the lightness in me that I didn't know existed before she came into my life that summer day. I fought what she made me feel, but it was no use. Love is like that. I couldn't deny it after only a few days of being around her.

I see the curtains flutter a little and smile. Maybe she can forgive me.

For a few long moments, I hold my breath as anticipation builds inside me. I used to play silly games while I watched her back in the beginning. I'd will her to come to her window and see me so I could know she wanted me as much as I wanted her. It was stupid, but after you sit in a car watching someone's house for hours on end, you begin to get a little squirrelly.

The curtains fall still, but there's no sign of Tia. I

should just march right upstairs to her apartment and explain how this is going to work. I'm going to stick around until the danger passes, so she has a choice: get used to me being around or fight me on this.

Either way, I'm going to protect her.

The lights go out in her living room, and then the entire apartment goes dark. Maybe she's stronger than I imagined. I'm probably going to have to do more to make up for leaving her last year.

With a sigh, I close my eyes and lean back against the seat as memories of us happy together filter through my mind. Entire days spent in bed just enjoying one another. Making dinner and loving cooking for the first time in my life. Tia surprising me with this watch for my birthday I still wear and then giving me a night of sex I'll never forget.

We were happy. If only I didn't have to leave her.

A knock on my car window startles me out of my happy daydreaming, and my eyes fly open to see her standing there glaring at me. She's still the most beautiful woman in the world, even when she looks like she wants to kill me. I don't care how she looks as long as I can see her.

I lower the window, and before I can say a word, she snaps, "You're pretty much just going to stalk me now? Good to know you never change. You can't sit here if you're going to do that, though. My neighbors will call the cops. This isn't like my old apartment.

People watch out for one another in this neighborhood."

"That's all I'm trying to do, Tia. Watch over you."

Her frown deepens when I say that. "I guess there's no point in telling you to go away. Fine. But I'm not going to be responsible for when the cops come and you have to explain why you're doing your best creeper routine."

"You could ask me to come up and stay the night," I suggest with more hope in my voice than I've heard in months.

The happiness I expect to see in her doesn't materialize. Instead, she sighs like she's carrying the weight of the world on her shoulders and shakes her head.

"We can't do this, Jaxon. You broke up with me. Let's keep it that way. As for me or my father being in danger, we'll take care of ourselves, so you can go back home and forget me like I'm going to try to forget you."

"You'll never forget me, Tia. Just like I'll never forget you. There's a reason you aren't with anyone and I don't even want to look at other women. We're meant for one another."

Those words don't make her happy either. "A killer with a heart of gold for a singular woman in this world. Is that what you're going for with all this meant for one another talk? I can't risk letting you back in,

Jaxon. You broke my heart, and I haven't forgotten that."

I reach my hand out the window and touch her arm. As always with Tia, a jolt of electricity shoots through the two of us, and she abruptly pulls her hand away.

"No. I can't take the chance this time. Go home, Jaxon. I wish you nothing but happiness. It just can't be with me."

When she turns away and starts walking across the street toward her apartment, I feel like someone's ripped my heart out of my chest. Again. It can't end like this. I never believed we were finished, even when I left her last year. I always knew we'd end up together, but right now I can't see how that's going to happen.

Unless I do something to make it happen.

Desperate times call for desperate measures.

CHAPTER SIX

axon

I'VE NEVER BEEN THIS FUCKING ANXIOUS IN MY LIFE. With every minute that passes and Tia still isn't awake, I worry I used too much of that shit Cason swears never fails to work.

Pacing back and forth in front of the bed where she sleeps, I regret listening to him. Even more, I regret having to take this drastic step. Why couldn't she just come with me? All I was trying to do was keep her safe. Christ, you'd think I was trying to hurt her.

At least I was able to handle her parents better. They're nice, and those kinds of people never dream someone is lying to them. Tia definitely comes by her trusting nature naturally.

They'll be enjoying a first-class trip to Italy that will keep them preoccupied and away from here for at least a month. I hope Ryker puts his plan into action in that time and gets rid of Victor. I can afford to keep them in Europe for longer than the next four weeks, but getting them to agree to it will be another thing entirely.

I stop at the foot of the bed and watch to see if Tia moves at all. Fuck. Cason told me this stuff would only last for a few hours. Did I give her too much? Damnit, she needs to wake the fuck up right now.

Another five minutes go by with no movement at all, so I walk around the bed and gently nudge her shoulder to move things along. At least that's what I hope it will do. Since I've never used this stuff before, I have no idea what the hell is going to happen.

She doesn't respond to the first nudge, so I give her shoulder another one. She's breathing. I can see by how her chest rises and falls that she's taking air in and letting it out.

So why the fuck isn't she coming out of it?

I return to pacing, hoping at any minute she'll wake up, but when ten more minutes go by, I can't wait any longer. I sit down on the bed next to her and give her a little shake. Nothing too much but hopefully enough to get her out of it.

Her eyelids flutter ever-so-slightly, but she still

doesn't wake up. Christ, am I going to have to take her to the hospital? That'll be fun. I'll have to pretend some asshole at a club drugged her so they don't arrest my damn ass right on the spot.

When I get my hands on Cason, I'm going to fucking smack the shit out of him.

I try again to shake Tia, this time a little rougher, and finally her eyes slowly open. I don't think I've ever felt so relieved in my life. My heart stops racing, and I sit back to take a deep breath.

"Where am I?" she quietly asks as she looks around the strange room we're in.

"It's okay. I'm here, Tia," I say, leaning forward to kiss her softly on the lips.

I never get to because she slaps me across the face so hard I nearly see stars. Falling back onto the bed, I shake my head as I rub the spot she hit. I had no idea she had it in her.

"What did you do?" she angrily demands.

Sitting up, I smile at her. "You're going to be fine. Are you hungry?"

Tia slowly lifts herself up and glares at me. "Am I hungry? You son of a bitch! You drugged me and kidnapped me, didn't you?"

I tilt my head left and right as I try to find the right words to say. "Kidnapped is such an ugly word. Let's say I did what needed to be done to make sure you were safe and leave it at that."

Her eyes flash pure rage, and she kicks her feet

against my side before swinging her legs off the bed. "The word is kidnapped, Jaxon. Don't try to sugarcoat it. I can't believe you did this! It wasn't enough that you came back and turned my life upside down. For days, I was looking over my shoulder wondering when you would show up. Let me guess. You got in when I left my front door unlocked that day I was bringing in groceries. Jesus, Jaxon. You promised me you'd never do anything like this. Remember that, or is that not something you want to talk about?"

Her legs give out as soon as her feet hit the floor, so I quickly scoop her up into my arms and set her back down on the bed. "We can talk about anything you want. I just need you to take things slow for a few minutes. By the way, when someone like me tells you you're in danger, leaving your front door open so anyone can walk in is exactly what you're not supposed to do."

She continues to glare angrily at me as she looks around the room. "Someone like you. A bad man is what you mean. Delightful."

There's no point in denying who I am. I'm a bad man. She's not wrong about that.

Rubbing her eyes, she angrily asks, "What did you give me? Where are we? I need to get out of here to see my parents. Or did you kidnap them too?"

I smile, hoping to defuse the tension between us. "No, I didn't kidnap them. They're enjoying a vacation to Italy. I hired a tour guide to take them to all the best spots, and they're going to be staying in first-class hotels all the way. Trust me. They're going to have a great time. They loved the idea. I took a shot that Italy would be a great place to visit for them, so I guess I got lucky."

Tia shakes her head and grimaces. "You should assume that's the last time you'll get lucky with anyone in my family. Now where the hell have you taken me? You know I have work. If I don't show up, they're going to fire me."

"I took care of that too. You're sick. Mono. Sucks, but you're going to need about a month to recover."

Confusion fills her expression, which is so much better than the pure anger she's been giving me every second since she woke up. "How did you do that?"

"I have a doctor who—"

Before I can answer, she shakes her head again and holds up her hand to stop me. "Don't bother. I don't want to know. I guess you figure since you have more money than God that you can just pull this kind of shit and everyone will be fine with it. So my parents are touring Italy for God knows how long, and I get to stay here in Chez Hostage with you. Well, forget it. Nope. Not happening."

She stands up again, and this time she doesn't fall straight to the floor, so she storms out of the bedroom. I follow and find her in the kitchen looking in the refrigerator. Good. I was thinking I might have to stop her from leaving the house.

"I can have something made for you. Just tell me and I'll get the cook to whip it up. She's quite good. My uncle found her in this tiny restaurant right outside of Baltimore slaving away for next to nothing and stole her away on the spot."

Tia leans back and looks around the refrigerator door at me like I said something bizarre. Her eyes narrowed to furious slits, she asks, "So is this a family trait? Stealing people away from their happy lives to come stay with you people? You should try a dog and leave us all alone."

"You know what I mean. The woman was working in a crappy job, so he offered her a job as a cook for him."

"Then what is she doing here? By the way, where is here? I need to know when I decide to leave."

I can't help smiling at how feisty she is right now. It's one of the million things I love about Tia.

"She's here because he didn't think I'd want to cook. He was right."

As she slams the refrigerator door shut, she mumbles, "How nice. Wealthy psychos."

"As for where here is, we're outside of Philly. It's a house that's in my family that they don't mind me using for my purposes."

Tia shakes her head in disgust. "Your money never bothered me before today, but I think it's pissing me off. You have houses at your disposal where you can take someone you kidnap and a cook who comes with the deal. How nice for you. If you don't mind, though, I'll be leaving. I have a life to get back to."

When she moves to step around me, I stop her by gently grabbing her wrist. I don't want to hurt her, but I can't let her leave. Not until I know it's safe.

She looks down at where my hand holds her arm and then up at me, her eyes full of rage again. "Let go of me. Now."

With a shake of my head, I give her my answer. "You'll stay here until you're no longer in danger."

"From the part of your family that doesn't have money to burn and chefs to steal."

I don't know why her attack on my family bothers me, but I snap back, "You wouldn't be in this position if you hadn't dated my cousin first, Tia. Don't blame me for your bad choices."

Her shoulders sag as I finish speaking, and she sighs. "Nice. How long have you been waiting to bring that up, Jaxon? Like anyone ever asks to be kidnapped twice."

"You weren't kidnapped the first time," I say, needing to correct her for some reason.

What the hell does it matter what she calls it? The end result is the same.

Once again, she's forced to stay with me, only this time it's because I can't bear the thought of her getting hurt because Victor wants to be an asshole to the rest of the family.

Tia frowns and sighs again. "Right. I was just tricked. This time is the kidnapping. Do any of the people in your family simply have normal relationships? Have any of you tried just meeting women in bars instead of spiriting them off and drugging them?"

I think about how Ryker got together with Kaia and Cason got with Lily and shake my head. "Not really. Occupational hazard, I guess."

She tugs her arm away and walks toward the living room mumbling, "I guess bad men don't do things like the rest of us. How lucky for me."

Once again, I follow her and hope we can move past this angry part of our time together. I know she still loves me. I just need to make her remember that.

"So you're not hungry?"

Spinning around to face me, she laughs. "I don't believe for a second you have a chef here to cook for us. I looked around that kitchen, Jaxon. Gorgeous, to say the least, with all the stainless steel appliances and that gas range that's definitely chef level, but there's no food in the damn refrigerator. Why do you feel you have to lie to me? Is it to make me think you're a nice guy? Because that ship sailed the moment you took me from my apartment and kidnapped me!"

So much for getting past the anger.

"She's at the store. You'll see when she gets back."

"Then why did you say she could whip up something for me if she's not here? You must think I'm a total idiot. I bet this kind of thing works with people who don't pay much attention to what's said around them. I'm not one of those people, you know."

I take a step toward her and stop when she throws me the nastiest look I've ever seen. "I know you're not. I promise I'm not lying. You'll see. And for what it's worth, I love that you're smart. I just think you could believe in me a little more. We were together for a long time."

Of course, she doesn't miss a beat before saying, "Until you broke up with me."

Jesus, I can't deal with this for the next month.

Throwing my hands up in the air, I say, "Fine. I broke up with you. Yes, I did that. I told you why, and whether you believe me or not, that's the truth. I'm not going to keep trying to make you understand. It happened and that's it."

As I talk, her expression gets angrier and angrier until I'm pretty sure she wants to hit me. Marching over to where I stand, she pokes her finger hard into my chest as she shakes her head.

"Nope. No way. You don't get to be like that, Jaxon. You were the jackass who left me, not the other way around. I'm not okay with the it happened bullshit. Own your behavior. If you're going to be a bad man, then be a bad fucking man, but don't expect me or anyone else to be okay with it."

I truly love this woman, but at this moment, all I can think of doing is stopping her from talking so at least she might be able to remember how much she loved me before we broke up. It's never going to happen if all we do is argue, so it's time for more drastic measures.

We stare into one another's eyes for a long moment before I lift her up and throw her over my shoulder. She wants me to be a bad man? Okay. It's my nature, so I'm all in on that.

She complains the entire way back to the bedroom, but I'm not listening anymore. It's time for me to remind her of one of the things that made us so great together.

CHAPTER SEVEN

ia

NO MATTER HOW MUCH I KICK AND PROTEST, HE refuses to put me down, and then he dumps me onto the bed like a load of clean laundry. He's out of his mind if he thinks this is a good seduction technique.

Jaxon smiles down at me as I scramble to get back on my feet. "Enough fighting. I'm tired of it."

The look in his eyes tells me he thinks we're going to sleep together in a few minutes. Terrific. He's officially lost his mind. That I know for sure now.

I'm being held hostage by an insane madman.

As he gently eases me back onto the bed, I say, "If you think for a second I'm going to sleep with you after you kidnapped me, you're crazy. Let me up so I can leave this place."

He ignores me and starts unbuttoning his white dress shirt. "Why do you insist on fighting this? You love me. I love you. Why can't you enjoy this time together without any distractions?"

My mouth drops open as shock at the way he looks at this situation fills me. "Do you hear yourself when you say things like that?"

My question goes unanswered as he tosses his shirt onto a chair in the corner of the room. God, he looks even better than I remembered. No! I can't let myself get sidetracked by his tattoos and muscular chest and washboard abs.

Closing my eyes, I try to stay strong, but this man has always had an effect on me. I need to think of something completely unsexual. That pimento loaf my mother loves. That show on Discovery with the doctor who always seems to be popping people's zits. Elon Musk. Guys who comb their hair over to hide their balding heads.

"I like that you're not fighting this anymore. We're making progress," he says in a low voice I know all too well.

That's how he sounds when he's hard as a rock and ready. God, now all I can think of is how good it feels when he makes love to me.

Zits. Musk. Comb overs. Pimento loaf.

Damnit, it's not working. Even thinking about those gross things isn't turning me off.

The first touch of his hands on my leg to slip off my yoga pants makes my body come alive. I must be insane. That's the problem. He's not the crazy one. It's me. It must be because only someone who's out of their mind would be aroused right now.

I open my eyes to see Jaxon crawling up between my legs. He's naked and his cock is rock hard.

And he looks incredible. Like always.

"You know, I love you in these yoga pants," he says as he runs his hands up over my thighs.

"They're new. You've never seen me in them before," I say, desperately trying my hardest not to be seduced by this man.

I shouldn't be. He kidnapped me. That was after he broke up with me and tore my heart out. And he didn't call even once for an entire year.

All of these things should make me hate him.

Jaxon dips his head to press a soft kiss just above my right knee. Looking up at me, he grins. "I didn't mean these exact pants. I just like you in yoga pants in general. They make your ass look incredible."

"Let me up," I demand in the strongest tone I can muster.

Shaking his head, he makes a sound that reminds me of a wild animal's growl. "No."

No? Who the hell does this man think he is?

I try to push him away, but he won't budge. "I hate you, Jaxon."

He shakes his head again and grins. "No, you don't. Now stop fighting this."

Frustrated, I try to keep control of at least myself. "Then I think you should know I wanted to hate you for a long time."

He plants another kiss an inch higher on my leg and answers, his breath against my skin like a whisper, "But you couldn't."

So cocky. It would serve him right if I did hate him.

If only I could.

"What makes you think that can't happen?" I ask as he begins to pepper my inner thigh with soft kisses that drive me wild. "By the way, men aren't the only ones who can sleep with someone they don't care about, you know."

As much as I wish any of that was true for me, I can't lie. There's always been something about Jaxon that I can't deny makes me want him.

He lifts his head and grins like he knows all of this. "Tia, you never got serious with anyone in the entire year we were apart. You couldn't because you still love me, which works because I never stopped loving you."

I want to be as cocky as he is, but it's not my nature. I like being honest with people I care about, and he's no exception.

Then I realize what he said about my never getting

serious with any of those guys I dated this past year and sit bolt upright. "Did you watch me while we were broken up?"

Sliding up my body, he doesn't answer my question. Instead, he tilts his hips and glides his hard cock between my legs, exciting me more than I want to admit.

When he leans down to kiss me, he whispers against my lips, "I couldn't stop myself. I needed to know you were okay."

He cups my face in his strong hands as I look up into his eyes and admit the truth. "I wasn't okay, Jaxon. You have no idea how lost I was all that time."

Sadness fills his eyes, but he wills it away with a smile. "No more being lost. I found you, and you're mine forever this time."

God, I should keep trying to fight him. Why can't I?

As much as I don't want to give in, I hear one word in my head and then it comes out of my mouth against my will. "Promise?"

"I promise, Tia."

His lips brush against mine before he kisses me long and deep, sending need coursing through my body. I dreamed of this moment for so long and doubted it would ever happen, and now we're here together in this strange place that reminds me of the house where we first surrendered to what we felt all that time ago. I forgave him for what happened there, and I can't help but forgive him for the year apart and even for kidnapping me.

That's what you do when you're in love with someone.

I feel his hips lift off me, and then a second later, he eases into my needy pussy, filling me completely like he was always meant for me and only me. Like every time we're together, the feeling is sublime. He slowly pumps into me, taking his time even though I see in his expression he's eager for much more.

Running my finger along the dark stubble on his jaw, I study his gorgeous face. He truly is stunning with those dark eyes that seem to hold all the secrets I've always wanted to learn and chiseled masculine features that hint at his ruthlessness.

"Don't hold back."

He stares down at me with such piercing intensity that I almost want to look away. "It's been a long year without you. I'm not sure I can be gentle if I loosen the reins on all my demons."

"I want you to, Jaxon. No holding back. I want this reunion to be as honest as we always promised we'd be with one another."

His hands slide up to my throat, and with his right thumb, he traces the outline of my lips. "I love you, Tia. I'm sorry I wasn't honest a year ago. I'm going to spend the rest of my life making it up to you, starting now."

When he kisses me, it feel the power of his

emotions and hope he feels mine. I cling to his body as he speeds up his thrusts and plunges into me. Quickly, it's like he's everywhere around me and inside me, consuming every last doubt I had about him.

About us.

He's the same man he's always been. Hard. Dangerous. Passionate. All the things I loved about him before remain, and if possible, have become even more intense.

My fingernails rake across his shoulders as my body takes everything he gives. He grunts with each time he fills me with his cock, an animalistic sound that thrills me. I've never loved anyone like I love Jaxon. I know all the bad he's done, yet I can't help but adore him.

His fingers tighten against my throat, but I don't fear he'll hurt me. I fear nothing when I'm with him.

Lifting myself off the bed, I kiss him, sliding my tongue over his to tease him because I know it never fails to get him even hotter. It has the effect I knew it would, and he begins to pound into me, his cock slamming into my body with wild abandon. Desire races through me with every hard thrust into my body, and all I can do is cry out for more.

"Don't stop!" I beg and pull my knees up to feel him as deeply as possible.

He slides his hand over to behind my ear and pulls hard on my hair. I love when he does that. It never fails to make me go wild.

I wrap my legs tightly around his waist to give him the hint I want to get on top. Like before, he understands and flips over onto his back. He looks up at me and smiles like a happy man.

"Feeling like you want to be in control?" he asks.

Rolling my hips, I lift off him for a moment before sinking back down and taking every inch he has. "Not exactly. You did that thing with my hair, and you know what that does to me."

He sets his hands on my waist and squeezes. "I knew it would get you even hotter. That's why I did it."

I press my palms against his chest and lean down to kiss him. "Some things never change."

Jaxon stuffs his hands into my hair and tugs hard, eliciting a moan from me as I ride him. "They better not because I love a woman who likes it on top. Let me see you ride that cock, baby."

He pushes me down hard onto him so nothing separates us. Running his fingertips over my abdomen, he smiles, so I look down to see the outline of his cock inside me.

"Now that's hot."

I try to lift myself up, but he keeps me still. "I think I need to be able to move to make everyone happy here."

"Well, I like how this feels."

As much as I want to see him happy, I enjoy the

feel of riding Jaxon's long, thick cock, so I roll my eyes. "What if I enjoy the usual way?"

With a shrug, he releases his hold on my hips and slides his hands up my body to cup my breasts. "Whatever you want, baby. I'll take you whichever way makes you happy."

I close my eyes and settle into the rhythm of our fucking. Beneath me, Jaxon groans and pinches my nipples.

"God, you feel so fucking good. I don't think I'm going to last for long, though. A year with just my hand has left me horny as all fucking hell."

Looking down at him, I don't analyze the truthfulness of his statement and take him at his word. I don't want to know if he was with anyone else. What happened in those months we weren't together doesn't mean anything now.

All that matters is he's back and I've forgiven him.

My orgasm begins to unwind deep inside me, so I ride him faster now, slamming my body down onto his cock in a desperate search for release. Jaxon sits up and wraps his arms around me, holding me close as I inch toward that delicious moment when I come.

"That's it, baby. Give me everything you have, and I'll give you all I am," he says low and deep in my ear.

I scratch my nails across the back of his neck, and he responds by pulling my hair. It's pain and pleasure mixed into one glorious feeling that sends an exquisite feeling straight to my pussy.

It won't be long until I come, so I hold on tightly to him, my hands grasping his muscular shoulders. We stare into each other's eyes, and the connection that's always been there between us makes me feel like I'm home.

His cock twitches inside me, and before I can orgasm, he comes hard with a loud groan. My body takes every ounce he has and then a second later, I come. My thighs shake uncontrollably, and although this feels incredible, I can't stop the tears that begin to flow down my cheeks.

I bury my face in the warmth of his neck, loving the smell of his skin. It's masculine with a hint of musky cologne like always.

The two of us fall still, and Jaxon softly runs his hand over my back. "Did I hurt you?"

Lifting my head, I smile and wipe the tears away. "No. I don't know why I'm crying. That felt incredible."

He smiles, and it lights up his dark eyes. "Good. I was worried I was a little too rough there. I know you used to love it that way, but…"

His sentence trails off to silence. I don't want him to be unsure of how I feel, so I kiss him and whisper against his lips, "I do love it that way, but only with you. I missed you, Jaxon."

I smile as he cradles my face and presses his forehead to mine. "I missed you too. I'll never leave again. I promise."

With a sigh of pure happiness, I rest my head on his shoulder. The past is gone. I can forgive him for everything, and our future together is all I've ever wanted.

"I love you, Tia."

I never thought I'd hear him say those beautiful words again, and now that I have, I don't think I could be happier.

CHAPTER EIGHT

 axon

TIA LIES NEXT TO ME WITH HER HEAD ON MY CHEST as I slowly remember the reason we're here. Nobody but Ryker and Cason know we're using this house, except the cook, but my uncle swears she's good. We just need to stay here until Ryker handles the Victor situation.

Not that it's a bad place to hang out for a month. Five bedrooms, six bathrooms, and ten acres of gorgeous land to explore isn't exactly slumming it. But to be honest, I'd rather be at Tia's apartment, even though it's cramped compared to this house. We don't need a cook or all these bedrooms, but mostly, I love that place after only one time being there because where she calls home I want to call home.

For now, that's just a dream of mine I haven't even shared with her. I'd give anything to be able to settle down like Ryker, Cason, and Kane. I can't, though. Not yet.

Maybe when this Victor problem is solved that will change.

Nothing would make me happier than being able to ask Tia to marry me. But I can't do that when my job is to be an enforcer for my family. That's no life for her or a kid, and whenever I think of us together in the future, it involves kids and a house where they can play and have the kind of childhood I never had.

As I daydream about that future for us, Tia lifts her head and smiles at me. "You're really quiet. Everything okay?"

I'd love to tell her about what I dream about for the two of us, but I won't. Not until I know there's a real chance I can give her the life she deserves. I won't make plans when it's far too possible I could be dead the next time I have to do a job.

Squeezing her to me, I answer her question. "Never been better, although I'm thinking it's nearly time we got that chef to wow us with something great to eat. Ryker raves about her, so I'm hoping she's as good as he says."

Tia's expression grows dark at my mention of the other person living in this house with us. "Are you sure she's not going to tell anyone I'm here? You don't even know her."

I nod, as sure about this cook woman as I am about everything else. "Ryker wouldn't send her here if she wasn't safe. Trust me. She's good."

As she returns to resting her head on my chest, Tia sighs. "Okay. I trust you, and if you trust her, then I'm okay. By the way, what is her name? We can't call her cook lady."

I smile at the thought of that. "Her name is Ivy."

For a few seconds, Tia doesn't say anything, but then she sits up and looks at me strangely. "Ivy? How old is this chef? I got the feeling she was older than someone with the name Ivy."

I have no idea what that means nor do I have a clue as to how old the cook is. I've only seen her a couple times since I brought Tia here, and I wasn't exactly paying close attention.

"Is there an age criteria for names? I didn't know."

Tia twists her face into a grimace. "You know what I mean."

"Actually, I'm not sure what you mean, but why don't you lie back down? I was enjoying how cozy we felt," I say as I pull her down toward me.

She resists, though, shaking her head. "What does this cook named Ivy look like?"

I shrug, unsure why we need to be talking about the person whose only job is to cook our meals for the next month. "Dark hair. Longish. Maybe to the middle of her back. I'm not sure. All the times I've seen her, she's been wearing it up in a ponytail."

Honestly, I don't think I've noticed anything else about her. Oh, yeah. There is that tattoo she has that's sort of cool.

"A ponytail?"

Nodding, I add, "Yeah. That's the only way I saw her spider tattoo on the side of her neck."

For some reason, Tia looks horrified. I don't think it could be the tattoo. I have dozens of them, and she's always liked them.

"A chef with a tattoo who wears a ponytail?" she asks in a tone that tells me none of that pleases her.

I shrug once more, still not understanding why we're bothering to talk about her. "I guess. She seems nice. You'll get to meet her when we get hungry."

To my surprise, she swings her legs off the bed and grabs her clothes to start getting dressed. "I think I'm hungry now."

"Really? I was enjoying us just lying here in bed."

As Tia tugs her black yoga pants up her legs, she says, "We can get back to that after we eat and I see this cook."

Ah, now I understand.

I slowly sit up, smiling because I get why she's so eager to meet Ivy. "You don't have any reason to be jealous, Tia. She's the cook. That's it. She makes our meals. Nothing else."

She shakes her head as she looks for her T-shirt.

"I'm not jealous. I just want to meet the person we're going to be sharing this house with. I'm curious. Where does she sleep?"

As I search for my pants, I answer, "I'm not sure. This is the first day I'm here, remember."

When she begins walking toward the door, I follow her, but before we get out to the hallway, Tia spins around and shakes her head. "You are not planning on walking around with just pants on. Where's your shirt?"

I look around and can't find it. "I don't know. I must have tossed it somewhere when I was getting undressed."

"You need to find it."

Sure what I need to do is make her see she's worrying over nothing, I pull Tia to me and kiss her long and deep. When I back away, I smile. "You don't have to worry, baby. I'm madly, crazy, out of my mind in love with you. I don't care about the cook my uncle hired to feed us. If you want, I'll call Ryker and tell him to get her out of here."

Oddly enough, that doesn't bring a smile to her face. Her frown actually grows deeper. "Don't be like that. Please, don't. You make me feel like I'm being stupid."

"No, you're being jealous, and I can't deny I like it. But you don't have to be."

Tia hangs her head and doesn't speak for a long

time. Finally, she quietly says, "I'm sorry. I'm being stupid."

"No, not stupid at all."

When she lifts her head, I see tears in her eyes. "Why are you crying?"

"Because I'm being stupid! Is there a better reason for someone to cry?"

I'm pretty sure there's no good response to that question, so I avoid answering by hugging her tightly to me. Against the top of her head, I say, "You're not stupid. You don't have anything to worry about, though."

Looking up at me, she says, "I guess I'm feeling insecure. You left me for a year, and then this happens, which I understand. I'm not angry about you bringing me here. Not anymore. I just find it strange that our first days together again are with some woman with tattoos named Ivy."

I brush her hair back to show her beautiful face. "I'll tell Ryker she can go back to the house then. I can cook. I know you can cook. We don't need her here."

Tia's blushes and her cheeks turn pink. "No, that doesn't sound right. Don't listen to me. I'm being stupid."

"Are you sure? I don't need her here. I have all I need right in front of me."

Standing on her tiptoes, she kisses me sweetly on the lips and finally smiles. "I'm sure. It's fine. If Ryker says she's that good, maybe we'll have some great meals."

"That's the spirit. Let's go grab a bite to eat and you can meet her and see there's nothing to worry about. I'm sure she's back from the store by now."

I take Tia's hand in mine and bring it to my lips to give her a tiny kiss on the knuckles. As we walk out of the bedroom, I nudge her arm.

"You're beautiful when you're jealous."

She glances over at me with a skeptical look in her eyes. "Only then?"

Wrapping my arms around her, I walk behind her and nuzzle the spot on her neck just below her ear. "No. All the time but when you're jealous too."

It's the sweet moments like this that I've missed the most with her. Sure, the sex is incredible, but when neither one of us is guarded and we let each other relax is when we're happiest together.

And then we turn the corner into the kitchen and I see Ivy standing at the island in nothing but a blue and white bikini that leaves nothing to the imagination. I feel Tia's entire body tense up and know this is going to be a problem.

Fuck. She has to go. I don't care how good her cooking is.

"Hey, Jaxon! What's up?" Ivy asks, and one look at Tia's expression tells me this is not going to go well.

CHAPTER NINE

ia

EVERY FIBER OF MY BEING GOES ON RED ALERT when I see this woman I have to share a house with standing in a barely-there string bikini that shows off her huge boobs chopping something on the island, and then when she speaks to Jaxon in a way that's nothing less than flirty, I'm definitely not happy. What kind of hired help hangs around looking like this? Shouldn't she be in one of those white chef's uniforms? Maybe not the big chef's hat but definitely more than the tiny triangles of fabric barely covering her bits and pieces.

The look on Jaxon's face tells me he's uncomfortable, but why? Immediately, my mind goes to a place I don't want to think about. Does he know her better than he tried to make it seem in the bedroom? Back there, he didn't mention anything about her having a smoking hot body. All he said was she had dark hair and a tattoo on her neck.

My eye is drawn to the black spider and spiderweb on the left side of her neck. It's an ugly tattoo that looks homemade. Why didn't he mention that? It's not like Jaxon doesn't know anything about tattoos. He has a ton of them.

He holds me close to him, resting his chin on my right shoulder as he says, "Hey, Ivy. I want you to meet my girlfriend, Tia."

The way she looks at me makes me think something is definitely off about this whole situation. It's not jealousy or anger I see in her expression, but I swear when she turned to look at me, she looked almost like she'd been waiting to see my face.

Why, though?

She wipes her hands on her bikini bottom and hurries over to where we're standing to shake my hand. "Hi, I'm Ivy! I'm here to cook you guys whatever you want, so your wish is my command. Just say the word."

The only words I want to say to this woman are go away, but I don't want to sound petty or jealous, so I plaster a smile on my face and say, "Hi, Ivy. It's nice to meet you. I hope you got something at the store because there wasn't a thing in the refrigerator when I looked before."

"I did. The fridge is stocked, and whatever you guys want to eat can be ready in no time. You name the dish, and I'll whip it up."

Jaxon hugs me tightly and in my ear says, "That sounds great, doesn't it? What would you like to eat? Feel like a big meal or just something to snack on?"

I look back at him and with my forced smile say, "Whatever you want, honey."

He's a smart man, so he picks up on my feelings quickly. He gives me a kiss and then turns toward Ivy. "What about French toast? That would be great."

The cook, who I thought just said she'd make whatever we want, gives him a strange look and laughs. "French toast? That seems like a weird thing to have in the middle of the day. What about a salad with some grilled chicken. I can have it ready in a few minutes."

I open my mouth to tell her I want the damn French toast, but Jaxon speaks before I can. "French toast is Tia's favorite, so just make the French toast. We'll be outside, so let us know when it's ready."

Without another word, he takes me by the hand and leads me out the glass doors to the patio in the backyard. When I look back, Ivy is busy getting things ready to make what we want. So much for her opinion.

Jaxon and I sit at the table with a big yellow umbrella to shield us from the sun, and for a few seconds, neither one of us says a thing. Finally, I touch his hand and smile when he looks over at me.

"Thank you for doing that."

"It was nothing. We told her what we wanted. I didn't want her opinion to go with our French toast. Just some syrup and butter will do."

He has no idea how much it means to me that he put his foot down and insisted on us having what I love. I want to tell him, but I'll leave that for later. Right now, I just want to enjoy this beautiful sunny day with him.

"I love you. Do you know that?"

That finally makes him smile. "I know. I still love hearing it every time you say those words, though."

"Good, because I plan on saying them a lot," I say with a giggle.

When we're like this—relaxed and sweet to one another—I'm happier than I ever imagined I could be. He makes me forget all the bad things in life, like the fact that someone is out to hurt me and my parents.

And what Jaxon does for a living.

Curious about them, I ask, "Do you get updates about my parents while they're in Italy?"

He nods and takes out his phone. Sliding it across the table to me, he says, "Check the messages for the name Albert. From what he's said so far, they're having the time of their lives."

I read through the four messages this Albert person has sent Jaxon in the past two days. My parents do seem to be having fun. They're in Venice to start the trip and have taken a gondola ride and visited Piazza San Marco. They're scheduled to have dinner later tonight at the best restaurant in the city.

When I finish, I hand the phone back to him. "What did you tell them about me? I'm sure the first thought they had was they would like me to join them."

He wraps his fingers around my forefinger in that way he always loved to when we would sit and watch TV. "I told them exactly who I am and that I would make sure you're safe no matter what."

"Did you tell them I'm in danger?" I ask as my heart clenches at how scared my parents must be if they know that.

Jaxon shakes his head. "No. I didn't think that was necessary. I think they got the feeling something was happening, but I promised them I'd take care of you. I had the sense they knew my name when I told them who I was. Did you ever mention me?"

I see the uneasiness in his eyes as he waits for me to answer. He's afraid I told them what happened when we met. He doesn't have to worry about that. I've never told anyone, not because I'm ashamed of anything but because I don't know if they'd understand how I could fall in love with him after those first days.

Nodding, I smile. "I told them I was dating

someone named Jaxon. Nothing else. I didn't care to say anything more."

"Because they wouldn't want you to be around me if they knew the circumstances of how we met?"

I lower my head to kiss his fingers still lovingly wrapped around my forefinger. "No. I don't care if people know, but I'm not interested in their opinions about it. I love you. That's all they needed to know."

"Did you tell them we broke up?"

"No. They probably guessed, though, since I was pretty down for a long time."

He leans back in his chair and closes his eyes as he turns his face to the sun. "I guess I should be happy your father didn't take a shot at me then."

That makes me laugh since I don't think my father has ever hit a single soul in his life. "My father's not like that. He might give you an angry look, but he's not a violent man, even when he's angry."

Jaxon turns his head and looks into my eyes. "What you mean is he isn't a bad man like me."

"My father is sweet and kind. Just the way my mother likes. Some women like sweet. Other women like bad. Good for you I have a thing for bad men."

His eyes get big, so I quickly add, "Well, just one bad man, if I'm being honest."

I guess I'm not the only one who's jealous.

"I'm thirsty. Are you? I'm going to run in and get a drink. Do you want something?" I ask as I stand to walk back into the house.

"Orange juice for you?" Jaxon asks with a chuckle.

"Good to know you didn't forget my favorite drink with French toast. Want some?"

He thinks for a few moments and shakes his head. "No, not orange juice. See if there's any soda."

I lean down and kiss his cheek. "Dr. Pepper?"

Turning his head to look at me, he smiles. "Good to know you didn't forget."

That year apart didn't change how much we know about one another, it seems.

I find Ivy standing at the stove finishing up our French toast when I walk inside. The warm scent of vanilla and butter fills the air and smells heavenly. As I head toward the refrigerator, she looks over at me and says, "Anything I can help with?"

"No, thanks. I just need to grab a couple drinks."

She didn't lie about filling the fridge. It takes a bit to root through all the food and drink to find Jaxon's favorite soda, but I spy it at the back of the top shelf. I grab the bottle of orange juice from the door and then it's a matter of locating a couple glasses.

Ivy watches me instead of paying attention to our food she's cooking while I'm searching through cabinets, so she points at the one on the far side of the room. "Glasses are over near the sink there."

I follow where she's pointing and find them just as she said. "Thanks."

After pouring our drinks and returning the bottles

to the fridge, I start back to the patio, but Ivy stops me. It takes everything inside to not ask why she's cooking in a bikini, but I choose to be nice and decide not to.

"You're very lucky to have a man like Jaxon. I can tell he's crazy about you."

Something in the way she says that hits my ears as part jealousy and part kindness, and I don't know which to pay attention to more. Her expression appears to say she's flattering me, so I nod and smile.

"Oh, I know. The French toast smells incredible. I can't wait to taste it."

With that, I head back out to the patio where he's enjoying soaking in the rays on this gorgeous day. I set his glass of soda in front of him and sit down.

"You know, Ivy thinks I'm lucky to have a guy like you."

He doesn't react for a long moment, but then he sits up and turns his chair toward the table and me. As he grabs his glass to take a sip of soda, he gives me a strange look.

"Okay. Not that she's wrong, but she knows this how?" he asks, arching a single dark eyebrow.

"She said she can tell you're crazy about me."

He's quiet for a few seconds after taking a drink of his soda, but then a smile lifts the corners of his mouth and I know he's not upset. "I don't know how. Maybe we give off a lovey-dovey vibe? Well, me. You've been pretty grim around her the whole time."

For a bad man, he really can be quite sweet at times.

"I had my reasons, but I swear I was nice when we talked inside now."

Jaxon shrugs and lifts my hand from the table to press a kiss onto my fingers. "I don't care if you're terrible to her. She's no one to me. Not that I think you could be. You don't have bitch in you, Tia."

That makes me laugh, even though he's not really wrong. "I don't know if that's a compliment or not. I can be pretty snarky when I want to."

Leveling his disbelieving gaze on my face, he shakes his head. "Baby, what you think is snarky and bitchy is nothing compared to some people. It's okay, though. You're nice. Nothing wrong with that."

I squeeze his finger tightly. "You make nice sound like a disease."

"Not at all," he answers with a sexy grin. "I think nice is hot."

We sit enjoying the warmth of the sun for a few minutes, but Ivy never comes with our food. The French toast should have been done by now. What is she doing in there?

Probably dancing around the kitchen in her bikini like some adolescent girl in a fucking rom-com.

"What's holding up the French toast?" I ask him after a while.

He looks toward the glass doors leading to the kitchen and shakes his head. "I don't know. How were things coming when you went in for the drinks?"

"It was almost done. I think your uncle may have been more impressed with her itty bitty bikini than her talent as a chef."

Jaxon throws his head back and laughs. "You don't know Ryker. Since he met Kaia, he doesn't even notice other women or their bikinis. I'll go in and check on our food. Maybe she's doing something special to the toast."

I watch him as he walks inside, and I wonder what the hell kind of special things can be done to French toast. You throw some vanilla extract into the egg and milk mixture, dip the bread, and cook it. There really isn't more to it than that.

It's not exactly rocket science.

A strange noise inside the house makes my ears perk up. Something about that chef rubs me the wrong way. I'm not sure I'm crazy about her being alone with Jaxon, so maybe I'll just head in and see what's up.

No, I shouldn't be like that. He loves me like I love him. There's no need to be jealous.

CHAPTER TEN

axon

WITH EACH STEP I TAKE, I GET MORE AGGRAVATED that this person whose only job it is to cook doesn't seem to be doing that. If the food was nearly done when Tia was inside talking to Ivy a few minutes ago, where the hell is it? I swear to God if I walk in there to find the French toast burning on the stove, I'm going to raise holy hell.

I push open the glass doors and walk into the kitchen. I'm greeted by the smell of burning food. Why the hell did Ryker think this person was a talented chef? The first damn thing she cooks for us she ruins. What the fuck?

When I get finished reaming her out, I'm calling him and demanding he call her back to whatever her usual job is for him. Maybe Tia's right about Ryker liking Ivy for more than her culinary talents. Nah, that's impossible. He's madly in love with Kaia, and they have little Maxim now. I've never seen him happier.

But whatever he thinks about this Ivy person is completely off the mark.

I hurry over to the stove and turn off the burner, but our meal is ruined. Fucking great. Ivy isn't anywhere in the kitchen and dining room area, of course. Why would a cook actually stay where the damn food is cooking? Seriously, this woman had one goddamned job.

Smoke fills the room, so I make sure the overhead hood is on to clear the place out. While that does its job, I begin looking for Ivy, who doesn't seem to be able to do hers.

I can't find her anywhere, which seems odd. In fact, all of this feels wrong. My gut tells me something is off, but I don't know what.

As I march around the first floor searching for her, a terrible thought crops up in my mind. Does Ryker know everything there is to know about this woman? Is it possible she's not who she says she is?

Then an idea comes to me that makes my blood run cold. Is she not a cook at all but someone sent by Victor to do the job he can't with Tia?

I run back outside to find her sitting like she was when I left a couple minutes ago. She looks at me with confusion since I'm sure she expected to see the food with me.

"What's going on? You look like you've just seen a ghost, Jaxon."

Taking her by the arm, I hurry her back inside. "Come with me."

"Why? What's wrong?"

The first step into the kitchen lets Tia know what's going on. "She burned the French toast? How hard is it to cook pieces of bread? Where is she? Maybe if she didn't bail on the meal it wouldn't be ruined."

I don't answer any of her questions because I need to find Ivy. Now.

When Tia tries to walk over to the stove, I refuse to let go of her. "No. You stay with me."

Fear fills her eyes, and she tightens her hold on my hand. "What's going on, Jaxon? Did something happen?"

"I don't know. Something is definitely wrong here. We need to find Ivy. I've checked all the rooms on this floor, so we'll go upstairs."

As we walk toward the stairs, she asks, "Did you check the powder room off the kitchen?"

I look at her and shake my head. "No. I don't think I've ever been in a powder room before."

Tia stares at me with eyes narrowed to slits and shakes her head. "It's a bathroom. Just a tiny one. She might be in there sick or something. That would explain everything."

Glancing around, I don't see a door that looks like it goes to a bathroom. "Where is it?"

Tia points toward what I thought was a closet at the end of the hallway. "Right there. Knock first, though. She might be dealing with something."

I have no idea what she's referring to, and I don't want to know at this moment. All I want is to find Ivy and send her back to Ryker.

After two raps on the door and no answer, I throw it open and hope I don't find her sitting on the toilet. The little bathroom is pitch black, so I feel around on the wall next to the doorframe and flick on the light.

There on the floor Ivy lies in a crumpled heap surrounded by blood. A slit across her throat tells me that's her blood she's soaking in.

Tia looks around me and screams. "Oh my God! Who did this?"

We don't have time to ponder that question. Someone got in here and killed Ivy, and they're going to be coming after us. I clamp my hand over Tia's mouth and shake my head.

"No more screaming," I whisper. "I need you to stay right next to me. Keep your eyes open."

I rush the two of us back to the bedroom to get my gun, and a few seconds later, at least I'm armed. The problem is I don't know who I'm looking for or even how many of them got in. I'm guessing a single assassin, but I can't be sure.

Before we leave to go search the second floor, Tia tugs on my hand and quietly asks, "Are we going to be okay?"

She stares up at me with tear-filled eyes, so I kiss her and whisper, "I told you I won't let anyone hurt you, Tia. Remember, I'm a bad man, so you're safe."

I get a tiny smile before she nods her head and takes a deep breath in. "Okay. What do we do?"

"We're going to search upstairs. My guess is they aren't still here, but we need to check."

I don't tell her what I'm also thinking. That the killer mistook Ivy for Tia. There's no reason why Victor would know there would be two women in this house. I brought Tia here under the cover of night, so no one would have seen her arrive. Anyone watching would think the woman they saw going to the store and doing the cooking was Tia.

The two of us slowly creep upstairs to where the other bedrooms are and check each one. There's no sign that anyone but Ivy has been up here. Clothes are strewn about her room, but all the other bedrooms are in pristine condition.

"Did someone rifle through her stuff?" Tia whispers as he head back downstairs.

I smile and try to make light of things to ease her worries. "Either that or she's a very messy person."

"She's dead, Jaxon. Maybe we should try to be nice."

"Sorry. Just trying to ease the tension."

We stop just before we get to the first floor so I can look around. I don't think they're still here. Good. But we need to get the hell out of this house now before they realize the mistake they made.

I guide Tia back to our bedroom and lock the door behind us. Pulling out my phone, I call Ryker to let him know what's happened.

"Enjoying your little vacation, Jaxon?" he jokes when he answers the call.

"Not really. Your fabulous cook is dead. She was making us French toast while we were outside enjoying the beautiful weather and someone came in and slit her throat before stuffing her in one of the little bathrooms. We're getting out of here, but you and the boys need to clean up and decide what you're doing with Ivy."

"Holy fuck! That bastard came after you two there? He doesn't even know that house exists. How did he know to find you there? Are you thinking he killed Ivy thinking she was Tia?" he asks.

I turn away from her so she can't hear what he's saying. "Yeah. That's why we need to leave because they're going to realize it sooner or later."

"Okay. I have another place I know he doesn't have a clue about. You two can go there."

Shaking my head, I smile at Tia as I say to Ryker,

"No way. Trust me. Victor knows far more than we thought. Today is proof of that. I'm not taking Tia to any place attached to you or the family."

"Where are you going to go then?"

That I don't know. All I know is if it's associated with anyone in our family, Victor likely knows about it.

We've clearly underestimated that son of a bitch.

"Not sure. I'll figure it out and let you know."

"Okay. Stay safe and we'll handle things on our end."

I want to suggest now is the time for us to move on Victor, but I don't say that because in the end, that's Ryker's choice. Killing your own brother isn't a move anyone makes lightly. Even bad men.

Stuffing my phone back in my pocket, I look over at Tia standing a few feet away near the dresser. She looks terrified. It reminds me of how she looked that week we met.

I walk over and cradle her face, wishing she didn't look so frightened. "It's going to be okay. We're going to take a little trip somewhere."

"Where?"

Of course, she would ask that. Always the curious one.

"I don't know. It's going to be okay. Do you trust me?"

Tia nods and gives me a tiny smile. "I trust you, Jaxon. I'm just scared."

Leaning in, I kiss her and whisper, "It'll be okay. I promise."

Now to figure out where the hell we can go to be safe.

As we walk out into the hallway toward the garage, she asks, "Do you think Ryker is right? That they thought Ivy was me?"

Damnit, I had hoped she didn't hear that, but since Ryker was practically yelling into the fucking phone, it's no wonder it came through loud and clear. I nod, hating that I have to tell her this.

"Yeah. One thing you should know about the guys who work for my other uncle. They don't tend to be the brightest bulbs in the box."

Tia sighs and tightens her hold on my hand. "Thank God."

I listen carefully for any signs that someone else is in the house with us as we hurry toward the garage, but the house is silent. We reach the car without any problems, so now I just have to figure out where we're going once we get on the road.

Just before we back out of the garage, Tia looks over at me and asks, "Are we safe for now?"

With a glance at the rearview mirror, I nod and press my foot to the gas. I'm guessing whoever Victor sent is miles away from here by now thinking he got the job done easy-peasy and now it's time for a nice cold one.

She breathes a sigh of relief as I turn the car

around and start driving toward the road, but out of the corner of my eye I see something racing across the front lawn. Before I can turn my head to see what it is, a gunshot shatters the driver side window, sending shards of glass everywhere.

As much as I want to take a shot at the fucker still running after the car, I need to get us the hell out of here. Asshole isn't much of a killer. The bastard completely missed me.

"Motherfucker! I swear to God when I get my hands on my uncle I'm going to be the one who kills him."

I speed down the road, my body full of adrenaline, and from next to me I hear Tia softly say, "Jaxon, it hurts."

Turning to ask what she means, I see the blood. That fuck didn't hit me but he got her in the arm. Her shirt is covered in red, and I can see by how pale she is that she's going into shock.

"I'm here, baby. Don't worry. I'll get you to a hospital and we'll have you taken care of. Just stay calm, okay?"

My heart's in my throat at the thought that Tia might die, so I floor it, sending dust and rocks up behind the car as I race toward the main road. I have no idea where the fuck the nearest hospital is, but I need to find one and fast.

Tia begins to cry and she sobs, "I'm scared, Jaxon. This hurts so much. I don't want to die."

I turn the car onto the road and jam my foot onto the gas again. Reaching over, I gently touch her cheek. "I won't let you die, baby. It's going to be okay."

She doesn't answer, and when I look over, her eyes are closed. "No. Stay awake! Stay awake for me. It's not long. I promise."

I see a car coming up fast behind me but don't pay it much attention since the woman I love is sitting next to me with a gunshot wound to her arm scared to death. Just as I'm about to bark out the question of where the nearest hospital is to the goddamned GPS, the car rams us from behind. I grip the steering wheel tightly to keep the car on the road, but when he hits us a second time, I can't stop it from careening into a field.

Tia cries out, and my head slams off the headrest, sending me hurtling forward toward the steering wheel. The car flips, and I can't stop it.

When we finally come to rest, Tia isn't making a noise and my head feels like someone has it in a vice. I need to get us the hell out of here, but when I try to start the car again, it won't turn over.

A woman's voice comes over the car's navigation system asking if we need assistance. "Yes! We just had an accident, and my girlfriend is hurt. We need an ambulance now!"

I gently touch Tia's cheek, but she doesn't respond. God, no. She can't be dead. I'm too afraid to check her pulse, though. I can't. She has to be okay.

Someone comes up to my side of the car, and I know before I even look it's no one who's going to help. I don't recognize the guy, but he looks like one of Victor's. Big, dumb-looking, and pointing a gun in my face.

"Time to go, Jaxon. Your uncle's waiting."

"No! Not without Tia. She needs help."

The guy gives her a single disinterested glance and shrugs. "She's dead, man. Brush it off because I'm not going to listen to you whine about some dead bitch the whole ride back."

"Fuck you! I'm not leaving here without her."

He rolls his eyes and lifts his arm. "Yes, you are."

A second later, he slams the gun into the side of my head. Everything fades to black, but the last thing I see is Tia slumped over in the passenger seat.

God, please don't let her die before the ambulance finds her.

CHAPTER ELEVEN

ia

I SLOWLY OPEN MY EYES AND TRY TO FOCUS, BUT instantly, my head begins to ache. Then my arm begins to throb like my heart has moved from the left side of my chest to somewhere near my right shoulder. Why do I feel like this?

"You're going to be okay," a soft feminine voice says beside me.

When I turn to see who it is, I'm greeted with a smile by a beautiful woman with dark hair and the kindest eyes I've ever seen. She looks at me like I mean something to her, but I've never met this person before.

"Your arm is going to be fine. The bullet went clear

through, which I'm told is a good thing. You were in a car accident, so you might feel sore all over too. Are you thirsty?"

As I try to take in all the information she's giving me, I suddenly remember about Jaxon. I sit bolt upright in bed, but it's obvious that's a mistake when I collapse back onto the pillows, instantly exhausted.

The pretty woman rushes over to my bedside. Shaking her head, she gently pats the sheets next to me. "Oh, I'm going to need you to stay lying down for a while. No fast movements like that for a little bit, okay?"

I nod, but I need to know what happened to Jaxon. "I was with someone in the car. Is he here?"

She shakes her head, frowning. "No."

When I try to ask her more questions, she walks out of the room, and I swear I hear her quietly sobbing. Is it that Jaxon didn't make it?

I rack my brain trying to remember what happened, but it's all a blur. I remember feeling something hit the side of my arm, and in an instant, my entire side felt like it was on fire. Then I remember Jaxon talking to me, but what he said is trapped somewhere in my mind.

My chest aches, but I don't think it's because of the accident. The thought that I won't ever see Jaxon again or hear him tell me he loves me makes my heart hurt.

Closing my eyes, I can see him as clear as day. His

dark hair and those deep brown eyes I swear could see into my soul. His tattoos all over his muscular body. His smile that always reminded me of a pirate's.

No! I can't think of Jaxon in the past tense. He can't be gone. I won't believe that.

"Tia?" a deep voice asks.

I open my eyes to see a man who resembles Jaxon. He's older, but he definitely looks like him.

"Who are you?" I ask as another man who reminds me of Jaxon steps out from behind the first man.

"I'm Ryker," he answers and tilts his head toward the man beside him. "And this is Cason. I'm Jaxon's uncle."

I may not be able to remember much of anything about the accident, but I remember Jaxon talking about his uncle. He had nothing good to say about him, and I think he said he wanted him dead. If I'm with him, then something very bad has happened.

Tears fill my eyes as he continues to explain something, but I'm not listening. All I can think is Jaxon's gone.

"Please don't cry. You're safe here," the older man says in what sounds like a kind voice.

"You're Jaxon's uncle," I say as I wipe my tears. "He's told me about you. He'd dead, isn't he? You killed him, didn't you?"

The two men shake their heads, and the younger one named Cason steps forward. "That's my father you're thinking of, not Ryker. This one's the good uncle. It's Victor Varens you need to be worried about."

For the first time since I woke up in this strange place, I feel like there's hope. But neither one of these men seem happy, which means it isn't all good news.

All I want to know is where Jaxon is.

"Tell me what happened to him. That's all I want. Did he survive the crash?" I ask, silently praying they'll say he's okay and somewhere I can see him.

Neither one answers immediately, sending my hopes crashing to the floor. "Just tell me! I'm stuck here in this place where I don't know anyone. I've been shot, for God's sake. Tell me if he's alive or not. At least give me that."

They stand there silently staring at me for the longest time until the older one finally says, "We don't know. He survived the crash, but my brother had one of his men take him. I'm imagining that's who caused the accident."

My mind races with a hundred questions. What kind of family is this that an uncle would kill his own nephew? How can we find out if Jaxon is alive or not? What are these men doing about finding him?

The younger man steps up to the side of my bed and smiles. "Jaxon told me all about you, Tia. I know he'd want us to take care of you, and that's what we're going to do. For what it's worth, I don't think my father wants Jaxon dead. Victor Varens isn't a good guy, by any means, but killing family isn't something he'd normally do."

I notice the older man named Ryker doesn't look so sure about what this man is saying, so I look at him and ask, "Why does it seem that you don't believe what this guy is telling me? I want the truth. That's all. If you think Jaxon is gone, then just tell me. I need to know."

He takes a few moments before he answers, "My brother doesn't value family as much as I do, but I think Jaxon's still alive."

I wait for him to continue, but that's all he says. God, the last thing I need right now is a man of few words. I'd give anything for someone to run off at the mouth at this moment.

"So you think he could still be alive? Why would your brother take him if he's family? I don't understand."

Sighing, he nods and then responds in a very measured manner that's making me want to shake him right now. "My brother and I are in a power struggle. He wants to head the family like he has for years, but I think business should be handled in a different way. That said, my guess is he will keep Jaxon alive."

I get the feeling he keeps the last words of that sentence to himself. For as long as he's useful. Or something like that.

The other man who said his name was Cason winces, which tells me I'm probably right.

"Do you know where he is?"

They both shake their heads but say nothing. I want to jump up out of this bed and try to find the man I love, and these guys don't seem to be much help. What I don't understand is why.

A second later, the kind woman who was with me when I woke up walks back into the room and stops beside me. "Guys, I think she's tired. Give her a little time to get acclimated to her surroundings."

Immediately, I notice the older one's expression softens when she speaks. The other one doesn't react, but I feel like he wants to say more and can't.

Or won't. But why?

"Kaia is right. You're probably not up to much talking right now. We'll continue this later," Ryker says before leaving and taking Cason with him.

"I was hoping to find out a little more from them," I say to the woman who I now know is called Kaia.

"Don't worry. They'll be back," she says with a smile. "Would you like me to open the window more? It's a beautiful day out today."

When I don't answer, she goes ahead and opens it, making the curtains billow in the breeze. I don't mind her wanting to make it nicer here for me, but I really wanted to find out more about where Jaxon is and what's happening to him.

"You know, Jaxon slept in that very bed last week. I woke him up and…"

She doesn't finish her sentence, so I quickly ask, "And what? Did something happen?"

I watch as her cheek's grow pink with a blush. Avoiding my gaze, she fusses with the comforter at the bottom of the bed and answers, "He wasn't wearing any clothes, and when I walked in, he was naked as a jaybird. That's what my mother used to say when my sisters and I walked around the house without clothes on. 'You're naked as a jaybird, Kaia! Get back in that room and get dressed this instant.' I guess she had a problem with nudity."

As I listen to her, I get the sense she had a problem with Jaxon's nudity. That makes me smile because the man has never enjoyed wearing clothes if he doesn't have to since I've known him. I swear he would be naked every minute of the day, if he could.

"That sounds like him. He'd get to my apartment, and I don't think an hour went by before he was walking around without a stitch of clothing on his body. I think he does that because he knows how good he looks."

Kaia smiles and shakes her head. "That might be, but I'm his aunt, and the last thing I needed to see was his business out there front and center."

Typical Jaxon. He probably felt not a hint of embarrassment either, if I know him.

"Let me guess. He just sat here in all his glory until you asked him to cover up, right? I think that man should work at a nude beach or something since he loves being naked so much."

She sits down on the bed near my feet and chuckles. "Ryker likes to tell stories about how Jaxon would always give his mother a hard time about wearing clothes when he was a little boy. He'd walk around the yard buck naked, and she always had to chase after him to put a coat on him. He tells that story much better, but it seems he's been like this his entire life."

After she finishes speaking, we sit in silence for a while as I think about the man I love out there God only knows where. Is he okay? Is he hurt? I know his uncle isn't a good man, but would he actually kill his own nephew?

As if she knows what I'm thinking, Kaia says in a low voice like she doesn't want the men in the house to hear, "I think he's alive and fine. Jaxon is tough. Yes, Ryker and Cason are tough too, along with all the guys they have working with them, but there's something about Jaxon that tells me he isn't going down without a hell of a fight. Stay positive. I know it's hard, but remember who he is. You'll be together again."

I take a deep breath in and let it out in a rush when my ribs send messages of utter agony to my brain. "I want to believe that. We weren't together for a year because of his job, and now he's gone again. I'm not sure I can deal with this if this is what life is going to be like, though."

Kaia nods like she knows what I mean. "You know, Ryker and I got together in what most people would call an untraditional way. I'm sure Jaxon has told you all about it, but I wasn't sure we had a future together either. Now we have our son and a life we're building here. It's not always easy. I had to come to terms with what he does, but I love him, so if that means I have to deal with things I might not like, that's life. That's what being in love is about, right?"

Even though I'm not sure I want to admit how Jaxon and I met, I say, "He held me hostage for a week when we met because he was doing a favor for one of his cousins I dated a while back. Let's just say we didn't have the best start to a life together."

She gently pats my foot before saying, "Same, although Ryker kept me captive for much longer than a week."

My mouth drops open in shock. "Is it a family thing? Is this how the Varens men meet women?"

She thinks about that for a moment before throwing her head back and laughing. "I think so. Cason, the other man you just met, got together with his girlfriend Lily the same way. They have a little boy now and are having another child in a couple months. So, I guess maybe it is a family thing. Not exactly the type of story you can tell friends and family, though, is it?"

I shake my head as I remember not telling a soul about how Jaxon and I met. "They wouldn't understand."

"No, they wouldn't. It sounds insane to say you fell for a man who did such terrible things. Yet, I can tell you from firsthand experience that I fell madly in love with Ryker. Same for Lily. Maybe the circumstances of your relationship aren't for everyone, but it can work. Don't count you two out yet. I believe you and Jaxon are going to be together again, and if you believe you belong together, then you'll make it happen."

The way she talks about things makes me think we're going to make it out of this current nightmare and be together. I'd always thought that Jaxon's job would be a barrier to a happily ever after, but maybe if Kaia and Ryker can do it, then we can too.

Assuming he's still alive.

CHAPTER TWELVE

axon

THE ROPE AROUND MY WRISTS BURNS EVERY TIME I try to move my hands, and the rag in my mouth to keep me from talking is about to make me puke. The asshole who pulled me from my car and left Tia for dead paces back and forth in front of me like he thinks I'm about to jump up from the chair I'm tied to and try to put up a fight.

I'm bound here, shithead. The only thing I'm doing until someone fucking unties me is plotting out your goddamned death with exquisite detail.

On top of the fact that I'm completely immobilized

is the other fact that the motherfucker is huge. He's got to be twice my size. What does he think I'm going to do even if my hands aren't tied together?

Without a gun, I'd be like a kid spitting at a damn mountain. I'm ballsy, but that would be downright stupid.

I don't know how long I've been here, but I'm guessing a few hours. That Victor hasn't come to see me yet means he's either playing one of his silly mind games or doesn't know what to do now that he has me.

Since my uncle isn't a great thinker, I'm torn between which it could be. He does like to try to fuck with people's heads, but that kind of shit only works on people who are afraid of him.

I'm not. Sure, he'll fuck me up pretty bad, but I don't see him killing me. He admires my skills too much, and offing family members is not something he likes to do.

In Ryker, I think that's a character flaw and shows weakness. In Victor, I applaud it since I think it's one of the few reasons I'll be able to walk out of here alive.

Well, walk might be too optimistic a description of how I'll be getting out of here, but I'm not thinking he's going to kill me. Just a little torture between uncle and nephew.

For the third time in the past fifteen minutes or so, I try to talk, but all that comes out is muffled gibberish because of the goddamned rag this asshole stuffed into my mouth. I've tried to spit it out, but the bastard wedged it in there so hard I'm thinking I'm going to be shitting out pieces of blue fabric for the next week.

The giant in charge of watching over me stops his pacing directly in front of where I'm sitting and glares down at me. "Stop making noise or I'll give you something to cry about."

Although he can't understand me, I say, "Smooth. Generally, somebody has to be crying to make another person threaten to give them something to cry about, but you do you, shithead."

I may have been mistaken when I thought he couldn't understand me because when I finish talking, he cocks his arm back and slams his fist into my left cheek so fucking hard I see stars. Mental note to self. Don't call this asshole names out loud unless I'm ready to get another beat down like the one he gave me when we first got here.

Good to know he can understand something, though.

Armed with that little nugget of knowledge, I say through the gag, "Is my uncle planning on just having me sit here and be bored to death? Is that how this is going to work?"

The stupid guy Victor employs to watch over me at the moment frowns and shakes his head before walking away. Maybe he only understands when people insult him. Odd talent, but I'm sure there are stranger things people can say are their claim to fame.

Well, I guess I'm going to have to take another one

on the chin to get something to happen here. Bracing myself for this guy's fist to connect with my face once more, I say, "Hey, shithead! I asked you if my uncle was planning to just wait until I get bored to death here."

Right on cue, the guy spins around and practically throws daggers at me as he marches back to where I'm waiting. I try to let my facial muscles go as slack as possible to avoid helping him to break my jaw, but this time he goes for my stomach, landing a punch so fucking hard he knocks the wind out of me.

So much for being creative in trying to get some answers here.

"Now shut the fuck up before I have to show you what's really up."

This guy is the worst at one liners, for sure, but he's got a hell of a punch. Thankfully, I haven't had anything to eat for so long that there was nothing to dislodge when his fist slammed into my body. Too bad, though. I would have liked to have covered him in some projectile puke.

I sit imaging the gag flying out of my mouth followed by vomit covering this douchebag for a few minutes, content to at least have that fantasy to sustain myself with for the time being. It's better than thinking about Tia.

Did the ambulance find her in time? Jesus, I hope to God the EMTs got to her before it was too late.

She's tough. She doesn't think so, but she's dealt with me, so she can get through anything.

As thoughts of her resting comfortably in some hospital somewhere make me happy, I hear the door behind me open. Is it another jackass underling like the one who's been pacing across the room for the past hour, or has Victor Varens finally decided to grace me with his presence?

I get my answer a few seconds later when my uncle's face comes into view as he walks around the chair and stops in front of me. Jesus, he looks like shit. Like the poster child for some fucking sexually transmitted disease. I guess that's what your face turns into when your entire family has abandoned you. And fuck, he's gotten fat. Too much good living for him has made him look like goddamned Humpty Dumpty.

Wait until I tell Ryker and Cason about this.

He just stares at me for a long time, so to get the ball rolling, I tilt my chin up to remind him I'm still gagged and say, "If you've come to talk, how about removing this thing first?"

Of course, he doesn't understand what I say since the fucking rag is in the way, but unlike his minion who's standing on the other side of the room now, he doesn't require me to insult him before he yanks the damn thing from between my lips. Thrilled I can finally take a deep breath in, I open my mouth wide and fill my lungs, letting it out slowly so as to not aggravate my ribs after that jackass probably bruised a few.

"Good to see you again, Jaxon. Life been treating you well?" Victor asks, acting like we're at some fucking cocktail party and we need to catch up.

"I'd say the same to you, but I'd rather be anywhere else but right here looking up at your ugly mug. Dude, what the fuck has happened to you? Is this what my future looks like? Because if it is, I'm going fucking vegan as of this very moment."

My uncle has always liked my smartass attitude, so I'm not surprised when he simply smiles and pulls up a chair to sit down in front of me. Victor is a dick of the highest order, but he appreciates the way I am.

He shrugs, but the smile never leaves his face. "Life is something you have to wear on the outside, Jaxon. Wait until you're my age. You'll get old, just like everyone else. Nothing you can do about that."

"Well, I do like a good New York strip from time to time, so I guess I'll be bagging that whole vegan thing."

"So, let's get down to brass tacks, shall we?" he asks, and all I can think is nobody uses the word shall anymore. Or brass tacks.

I don't bother telling him that, though, and nod my agreement since sitting here with my hands tied behind my back is getting old. "Yes, let's."

"That brother of mine seems to think he should

take over the family business. Don't bother pretending that isn't what he's thinking. I know Ryker far too well to not see the signs."

Again, I nod. "True."

"What baffles me is why he hasn't made a move yet. Can you explain that to me? Because if it was me, I would have taken care of business the moment the idea to take over popped into my head."

He's full of shit, and he knows it as well as I do. If that were truly the case, he would have put a hit out on Ryker by now and he would have had his own son killed. He can't be okay knowing Cason is working with the man who wants to see him gone from this world.

Now's not the moment to discuss that, though.

"You know Ryker. He's all about family."

Victor smiles before rolling his eyes. "It always was his weakness. How's that woman and the baby doing for him? I thought he'd be single forever, to be honest. Good to see him finally doing what he should have years ago."

"They're fine. He's all about that little boy. A son. You know how it is."

I watch as a darkness passes over his expression for a brief moment before disappearing. Of course, he knows. He had two sons. Michael's dead, and Cason now works with his enemy. Not exactly the track record of a great father.

"And Cason? How is he?"

"Good. He and Lily are expecting their second kid to give Lukas a brother or sister."

Why he's asking me these questions is beyond me since he must know the answers. It's not like he doesn't have people watching us like we have watching him.

"Hmmm. Not sure I like the idea of being a grandfather again, but I guess I don't get a say in that," Victor says in a voice full of what sounds like regret.

For what, I have no idea. He's done some pretty shitty stuff in his life, so I can't think being a grandfather is that bad.

My uncle strokes his chin and purses his lips like he's deep in thought. Since this is Victor Varens in front of me, that's highly unlikely. He doesn't have morons working for him out of chance. He collects these jackholes because he sees something of himself in them.

I wait, assuming what he's about to say is going to be something either incredibly stupid or stupendously ridiculous. Either way, I'm not pulling any punches with him. I don't believe he's going to kill me, so a little more torture from his flunky over there won't be too much for me to handle.

Finally, he sighs loudly, and I know he's figured out what he wants from me.

"So, tough luck about that girlfriend of yours, huh?"

He watches me closely to monitor my reaction so he can see if he's hit a nerve. It's almost insulting that he doesn't think I know what he's doing. The fucker was the one who taught me the job. Does he think Tweedle Dum over there beat my memories out of me?

"You're wasting your time, Victor. If all you have is dangling my girlfriend's death in front of me to see if you can get a reaction, you better go back to the drawing board and figure out a better tactic."

Merely saying the words my girlfriend's death makes my chest hurt, but I don't let him see that. If he notices even a tiny twitch in my expression, he'll exploit it for all he's got. I know how this works. Fuck, I've done the same thing myself. You'd think he'd remember that.

See, that's the problem with this guy. It's where Ryker has it all over him in spades. Yes, Ryker is a softer touch when it comes to business, but killing everyone who pisses you off is no way to run things. Being civilized never hurts a man, but Victor here didn't get that memo, so he's still living like it's the goddamned stone age.

He hums for a moment, processing my answer and wondering if it's simply bravado, no doubt. Then he says, "I thought you cared about that girl. I know Michael did. At least for a little while until I made him see he had a world to conquer and one sweet piece of ass wasn't going to be enough for the future head of the Varens family."

I smile, trying not to laugh when I say, "How'd that work out for him?"

The fact that he's dead and conquering nobody answers that question.

"The same way it's going to work out for you, son."

Shaking my head, I work to keep my temper under control. "I'm not your son. I'm your nephew, and to be honest, someone who's tired of these fucking games you're trying to play with me. If you're going to do something, fucking do it. Stop pissing around."

I probably let out a little too much of my emotions in that little speech, but to hell with him. I don't believe for a goddamned second that Tia is dead, so whatever he thinks he's going to do to me by claiming she is means nothing. And bringing up his son who happened to date her before me is bullshit, and he knows it.

Victor leans back in his chair and folds his arms across his chest. "Direct and to the point. I like that. Fine, here's how it's going to work. No, I don't want to kill you. I want you to kill someone for me. And no, not my brother or Cason."

I'm intrigued. He wants me to be his killer but not for the two people I thought were top on his list. Who does he want taken care of?

He stands and points at the shithead across the room. "Dickie here will give you all the details. Do what I want, and you'll be free from me for the rest of your life."

I'm barely listening after hearing my tormentor for the past few hours was a guy named Dickie. "Are you serious? Dickie? So I guess I wasn't wrong when I was thinking he was a dick."

"Funny. Just do as I want and you're free and clear."

My uncle begins to walk away, but I say, "That makes no sense. You know what's going to happen, Victor. Letting me go isn't going to stop that. What are you doing?"

"I have a job for you to do. You want to do this to stay alive. It's that simple. So do it and move on with your life. Find a new girl. Have some kids. Buy a house and get a nice lawnmower to take care of the grass. You seem like the kind of guy who thinks that's the type of life you want, so I'm giving you a free pass to go get it. Just kill this one person and you're out."

None of what he's saying makes sense. I'm sure when I hear the name it's going to be Ryker or someone else in my family I care about.

"And if I refuse?"

Victor smiles. "Then I'm going to let you walk out of this house, and by the time you get to the street, Dickie here is going to put a bullet into the back of your head. And before you say you know I don't want to kill you, that's true. I don't. But I will if you don't do what I want."

Typical Victor. He won't kill me because of how much he loved my father, but he'll have someone else do it so he can feel like he had no part in my death.

"Fine. Who is it you want me to take care of?"

He walks back to stand in front of me and gives me one of those crocodile smiles I know so well from him. I swear to God this guy gets off on this shit.

"Well, since your girlfriend is dead, you won't have any problem killing her father for me now, will you? Remember, this is your ticket to freedom, Jaxon. That's what you want, isn't it? It's why you walked away from that pretty girl from North Carolina. You can't have her, unfortunately, but you can have another one, and let's be honest here, man to man. One woman is as good as another. They're all the fucking same when they're on their backs with their legs in the air."

My emotions begin to get all tangled up inside me, threatening to expose how I truly feel about the possibility of Tia truly being gone and my killing her father as a favor for this fuck. I can't let him see any of this bothers me, so I shrug and put on my best expression of disinterest I can muster.

"Fine, but don't you have your own people to do this for you? I recall hearing you had a whole new group of guys working for you now," I say as casually as possible, looking over at the idiot Dickie to make my point.

Strangely, my uncle can't seem to control his own

emotions and rage practically explodes out of him when he answers me. "I did, but the people who I assigned to kill your girlfriend's father couldn't handle the job. Too bad. They would have had a future in my organization. Now all they have is a mouthful of fucking dirt where I had the two of them buried."

Too bad for Dash. Poor fuck. I only met him that one time in Ryker's office, but he seemed okay. I didn't know the other one, but that's what happens when you get mixed up with the likes of Victor Varens.

"So do I have Dickie put a bullet in your fucking brain, or are you going to man up and do this one last job for me so you can go live the bucolic life full of gardens and playdates for future rugrats? The choice is yours, Jaxon."

For a few seconds, I wonder if I can kill Tia's father. If she's gone, then her parents will be despondent. Maybe it would be a favor to them and put them out of their misery. It's not like I'd have to look hard to find them either. They're still in Italy on my dime.

"Okay. I'll do it. I have to say, Victor. I feel like you've gotten soft in your old age. Going after nine-to-fivers now? What happened to aiming for the big fish in our world?"

He stares down at me and smiles. "You mean like my brother? It's not something I even consider lightly, believe it or not. Family is off limits, usually. For Ryker, though, I may have to make an exception."

Fucking Ryker should have killed this motherfucker months ago. If he had, I wouldn't be sitting here with the tang of my own blood in my mouth and Tia's father's life wouldn't be in danger.

But most of all, Tia would still be alive and mine.

CHAPTER THIRTEEN

axon

THE GATES TO THE ENTRANCE OF RYKER'S ESTATE loom large in front of me after I had to walk here. Fucking Victor! I have no idea where my cell or my gun are, and I didn't have a goddamned dollar on me when he and that Dickie asshole tossed me out the back door of his town car about a mile away from his house.

He didn't kill me, but he might as well have now that he's saddled me with the job of killing Tia's father. How the hell am I going to do that?

The guard looks me up and down like I'm some

bum off the street, but before I can say a word, he finally recognizes me. "Jaxon? Is that you?"

I run my hand through my hair and exhale my disgust that even the guard at Ryker's house looks at me like I'm a fucking mess. "Yeah. I need to get in there to see Ryker."

The guard, whose name I can't remember right now, waves me through, and I start walking up to the main house looking like ten bags of smacked ass. Not surprisingly, Ryker comes hurrying toward me, followed by Cason and Kane not far behind.

"Come to see the shitshow?" I ask as they stop to meet me.

"What happened to you?" Ryker asks and tries to put his arm around my shoulder.

No fucking way. If he had done what he should have before now, none of us would be in this position. I'm not interested in having a family reunion with him after what I've been through.

Pushing him away from me, I say as I continue walking toward the house, "Well, your safe house is anything but safe, asshole. That chef you liked is dead, but you already know that. Thanks for nothing. One of Victor's idiot minions ran us off the road. A guy named Dickie, if you can believe that shit. I got to spend a nice few hours getting my ass beat by said minion, and then I got to hang out with your brother, who if you had handled your business before this, none of this would have happened. So even though I came here to see you, this is more to tell you fuck you, Ryker."

I glance back and see my uncle standing a few yards back like he's shocked I said any of that. Kane and Cason look equally as surprised.

Well, fuck all of them. They didn't take care of business, and I've had to pay the most for their feet dragging.

"Jaxon, wait!" he calls out, but I'm not listening.

I've heard enough of his excuses. Now I have to do a job that's tearing me up because he couldn't kill his own brother, a man who would certainly put a bullet in his brain if he had the chance.

Behind me, I hear the three of them grumbling about something, and it takes every ounce of strength I possess to not spin around and bitch them all out. I'd probably say something I'd regret later, though, since this part of my family I actually like, so I keep my mouth shut and storm up the drive to the front door where Kaia is staring at me in horror.

I catch a glimpse of myself in one of the windows as I walk toward her and realize I look much worse than I thought. No wonder the guard barely recognized me. The left side of my face is all swollen, and my right eye looks like someone pressed an unbaked biscuit into my eye socket. Dried blood sits under my nose and around my mouth, and my neck looks like someone's had their hands wrapped around it trying to kill me.

Not exactly my best look, but I don't care. I just want a hot shower, some food, and a bed where I can sleep for a few hours before I figure out what the hell I'm going to do to get Victor off my fucking back.

"Oh, Jaxon! You look like you've been dancing with the devil," Kaia says in that sweet way that usually makes me smile.

Now, it's the last thing I want to do as I pass by her. "Not now, okay? Your husband's inability to handle his shit has made my life hell, so I know I'm being a bit of a dick here since it's your house, but could you and everyone else just leave me alone for a while? It's been a rough day."

"But…"

I wave her off as I climb the stairs to that room where I slept the other night. God, that seems like it was forever ago when we were all drinking and having a good time.

"Jaxon, wait!" Ryker barks behind me, and for a fleeting moment, I consider marching back down the fucking stairs and letting him have it. Both barrels.

I don't, though. Yes, I have every reason to be royally pissed. The woman I love is either dead or somewhere at some hospital nowhere near where I am at the moment. I'm supposed to kill her father. I'm beat up to fucking hell. And all of this is because Ryker didn't kill Victor months ago.

That said, I'm nothing if not loyal, and I threw my lot in with Ryker when I had to make a choice between my uncles. I can disagree with Ryker about what he should have done to handle Victor before this, but he's still my boss.

Even if I want to knock him the fuck out right now.

So I ignore him and keep walking to that room, desperate to lay my head down for just a little while. If I can get even a few hours of solid sleep, maybe my life won't seem so fucking terrible when I wake up.

I feel my eyes closing even as I walk. Well, just my left one since my right one I can't even see out of it's so fucking swollen. I hope I get the chance to give that Dickie payback sometime soon. Let's see how he likes me shoving my goddamned fist into his face.

"Jaxon, wait!" Kaia calls out as she rushes down the hallway to stop me.

I like my aunt. I really do. But right now, all I want to do is snap at her to leave me the fuck alone. Do these people not understand what I'm going through? I've lost everything. At least give me a chance to recuperate a little before I have to deal with it.

She catches me just as I'm about to walk into the bedroom. "I need you to know something before you go in there."

"What? Like I should wear clothes this time so I don't flash you like I did last time? Fine. To be honest, I wasn't even going to change, so assume those sheets you have on the bed are going to need to be bleached to hell since I'm bloody underneath all this."

She seems uninterested in me, oddly enough, and instead looks at the door like there's something in that room I can't see. Did she change the kid's room to this one, and I'm about to walk in on Maxim taking his nap?

"Listen, Kaia. It's been the day from hell. I don't want to talk about anything right now, okay? I'm about as down as a man could be, and in addition to the shit you can see they did to me, I'm pretty sure I've got at least a few bruised ribs. Maybe even something going on with my spleen. So whatever it is you want to tell me, I don't care. In fact, I'm so fucking low at this moment, I don't care about anything."

Frowning, she looks like she's going to cry when she opens the door for me. "It's not all bad, honey."

She has no idea how fucking awful it is to be me right now.

I walk past her without a word into the bedroom and wonder why in the middle of the day it's so damn dark in here. Not that I mind. It's definitely better than the other day when Kaia came in and proceeded to try to kill me with sunlight.

As I strip out of my clothes, I silently chastise myself for blaming her. It was the hangover, not her who was trying to kill me.

But I'm an ornery motherfucker. I don't die that easily.

I catch a whiff of a familiar fragrance, but I push that out of my mind as quickly as it appears. That perfume Tia wears that smells like flowers in the summertime is probably similar to the detergent Kaia likes to use on the sheets. I can't remember the name of it, but it doesn't matter.

It'll be nice to be surrounded by something that smells so much like home.

Undressed, I throw back the covers, and the scent grows even stronger. There, in the dark, I tear up. Christ, is she dead, and I'm just too stubborn to admit the truth? If she is, it's my fault. I broke up with her last year to save her, and what ended up happening?

The same fucking result anyway.

God, it's days like this that I fucking hate my life. Why couldn't I have been born into a family of landscapers or tailors? Hell, I'd take a family full of fast food employees if it meant I'd get to have her in my arms again.

I sit on the edge of the bed as the misery I've been denying washes over me. Tia's gone. I fucking lost her because of who I am. Everything I worried about the entire time we were together happened, and there wasn't a damn thing I could do to stop it.

Behind me, I feel something push against my back. Did someone leave a laundry basket on the bed? That would explain why I'm smelling that summery flower scent. It would also explain why Kaia was in such a hurry to catch up to me. She could have just said there was something on the bed.

"Who's there? Kaia? Is that you?" a soft voice asks.

I jump up, stunned it's a person and not a basket full of fucking sheets next to me. I hurry to turn on the light and nearly fall over when I see her.

Am I dreaming? Did that shithead Dickie beat me up so badly that I'm hallucinating? Is it possible Victor didn't let me go and I'm still tied to that chair in his house getting the tar kicked out of me?

"Tia? Is that really you?" I ask, sure I sound like a fucking madman who's losing his mind.

She stares at me like I'm a stranger, which makes me sure this is some fantasy I'm playing out in my head as I get pummeled by Victor's henchman. Tia's dead. She's not here. Fuck, I'm not even here.

Finally, the vision I've created in my mind says, "Jaxon! You're alive!"

I shake my head to dispel this dream. It hurts too much to deal with right now. "This isn't real. I'm not really here, and neither are you."

Closing my eyes, I lean back against the doorframe and can't help but notice how real that feels against my shoulder blades. That Dickie must have fucked me up pretty good if I'm able to come up with a dream like this.

Maybe I'm in a coma. I saw something once on TV about a guy who was in a coma for years, and the whole time he was lucid and thinking of a million things. At the time, I thought that sounded pretty damn interesting, but now that it might be happening to me, I'm not at all thrilled about it. This is fucking torture thinking my dead girlfriend is sitting in the bed in front of me happy to see me.

She slowly sets her feet on the floor and walks around the bed to come toward me. This all feels so real. How am I thinking this up in such detail?

"Jaxon, what's wrong? It's me. Tia. Oh, baby, you look like a truck hit you. Are you okay?"

I stare at her for what feels like forever before she reaches out to gently touch my face. Her palm cradles my cheek, and as much as I know this is a fantasy, I don't care. I want to feel her caress me like she always did. If this is all I can have of her, then I'll take it. I don't care that it's merely a delusion.

"I'm so sorry, Tia. I tried to keep you safe. I did. I'm so sorry, baby. I failed, and I'll never forgive myself. I want you to know that. No matter how long I live, I will never forgive myself for what happened to you."

As I watch her smile, she leans in to me and softly kisses my lips. God, please don't let her disappear right now. Just give me a few seconds of this dream before she vanishes from me.

"I'm okay, Jaxon. Kaia and Ryker brought me here. My arm hurts where the bullet went through, and I'm a little banged up from the accident, but they say I'm going to be fine. I'm more worried about you. What happened? Who did this to you?"

I shake my head when the fantasy becomes too much for me to handle, closing my eyes so I don't have to watch her fade into nothingness. Taking a deep breath that hurts my ribs so fucking bad, I remind myself this isn't real.

"Honey, why won't you look at me?" she asks, and I swear my chest tightens at the sound of her voice now.

"Because you're not here. You're dead. Maybe I'm dead. I don't know. All I know is you're a fantasy I'm making up because I miss the real Tia."

"Open your eyes, Jaxon. I'm here. I'm not a dream. Honest."

I slowly lift my eyelids, expecting to feel the rush of disappointment when she's not standing in front of me anymore. That doesn't happen, though. I open my eyes, and she's right there smiling at me.

"This can't be. Victor told me you're dead."

She leans in and kisses me softly again, sighing against my lips. "I'm very much still alive. I promise. You can believe me, Jaxon. I've never lied to you before, have I?"

"No," I answer, swallowing hard as my emotions begin to unravel inside me.

"I'm so happy you're here. You look like you had to fight through an entire army to come back to me, though. Are you okay?"

Tia begins to look like a reflection in a pool as my eyes fill up with tears from how happy I am to see her again. I finally reach out to touch her, and she's as real as ever.

My Tia.

"I thought I was dreaming you were here. Then I thought I must be dreaming I'm here and instead I'm still back at my uncle's getting beat to hell. He said you died. I didn't want to believe it, but I saw you sitting there in the car right before one of his guy's knocked me out, and you were unconscious. I didn't know if the EMTs got to you in time. I'm so sorry, Tia. I never wanted you to be hurt by what I do."

Tears begin to stream down her cheeks, and when she kisses me, I can taste the saltiness on her lips. "I know. I know. But I'm okay. I never thought I'd be tough enough to handle being shot, but I guess I'm stronger than I ever thought."

Glancing down at her arm, I see the white bandage around her bicep. "I would have taken that bullet if I could have. I hope you know that. I'd take anything if it meant you not getting hurt."

She cups my cheeks and smiles. "I know, baby. It's not so bad, though, and I'm actually getting used to the pain, believe it or not. Now come over to the bed and lie down. You look like you need to sleep."

After turning off the lights, Tia takes my hand and leads me over to the bed. Every inch of my body aches, but just knowing she's alive and with me again makes me feel like I could take over the world.

As I slowly lean back on the pillow, she rests her

head on my chest. I hear her let out a heavy sigh, and I wrap my arm around her, loving the feel of her body against mine.

"I thought you were dead," she whispers against my skin. "I was lying here for all that time thinking I don't know if I can go on if you aren't in the world with me."

I know exactly how she feels. The thought of going on without Tia rang hollow to me every time I tried to come to grips with her being gone. She's my everything, and living in the world without her felt wrong.

"When he told me you were dead, I didn't want to believe him," I say in a low voice into the darkness surrounding us. "All I kept thinking was he was saying that to hurt me, but in my mind, I saw you sitting there in the car bleeding and knew it was possible you didn't make it. I've never felt so lost in my life."

She presses against me, and then I feel her lips brush against mine. "No more talking about us not being together. We're here, and we're safe. That's all that matters."

As much as I want to stay awake and tell her how much I love her now and forever, I can't keep myself from drifting off to sleep after all those hours of being smacked around by that asshole Dickie. I let myself go, knowing when I wake up my Tia will be right here next to me.

Just as it always should be.

CHAPTER FOURTEEN

ia

FOR THE PAST HALF HOUR, I'VE WATCHED JAXON next to me, amazed at how someone so rough could look so peaceful and innocent as he sleeps. I truly didn't want to believe he was dead, but as I lay here all day, I was beginning to lose hope.

I should have known better. Jaxon isn't a man anyone can get rid of that easily.

The bruises all over his face and body tell the story of what he went through after they pulled him from the car wreck in that field. I don't know his uncle, but from all he's told me and what I've heard from Ryker and Cason, Victor is a terrible man. That he'd hurt his nephew like this just makes that fact all the more vivid.

With my fingertip, I trace a deep purple mark across the middle of his stomach and wonder what he endured to get it. I hate to think of someone slamming their fists into his body. What could he have done to warrant such barbaric behavior?

"That tickles," he says with a chuckle.

I look up at his face and see him smiling. "I'm sorry. I didn't mean to wake you up. I just can't sleep anymore, but I didn't want to leave your side. I didn't want you to think I was all a dream."

"You are a dream, but the kind that actually exists. Trust me. The rest of my life is a total nightmare, so you must be a dream."

Sitting up beside him, I touch his hands covered in cuts and bruises. "You sleep like an angel, even though you look like you've gone twelve rounds with someone today."

He groans as he tries to push himself up against the pillows. "A shithead named Dickie. I swear if I get the opportunity, I'm going to give him everything he gave me and more."

I don't know if I should ask any of the questions swirling around in my head about what's going on, but I can't stop myself. I'm in the middle of all of it now, so I want to know what's going to happen.

"Jaxon, why did your uncle have someone do this to you?"

He tries to take a deep breath but stops halfway through and groans again. "Fucking ribs. God, they hurt."

Sensing he wants to avoid this conversation, I drop the topic for the time being. We can talk about everything later. He might not want to, but I need to know what the future holds.

When I don't say anything, lost in thought about the idea of a future with Jaxon, he says quietly, "My dear uncle Victor wanted to drive the point home that he has the power and I was just an unwelcome guest in his house."

His vague answer confuses me, so I ask, "What do you mean? You're his nephew. Why aren't you welcome in his home?"

Jaxon smiles and rolls his eyes. "My family isn't like yours. You come from nice people. I come from killers. And when killers want to get their point across, they either murder someone or give them a taste of pain. Since my uncle has some strange familial feelings about me, likely because of my father and nothing I've ever done since I betrayed him by coming to work for Ryker, he chose not to kill me. But he needed to get his point across, which meant Dickie and his fists of fury."

He's trying to be tough, but I know he's hurting. Not just physically either.

"I'm afraid, Jaxon. If he would do that to you, what would he do to me or my parents?" I ask as I stare at that terrible purple mark that seems to be getting darker as the seconds tick by.

When he answers my question, I hear fear in his voice too. "He'd kill you. It's that simple."

Hearing that sends terror coursing through me. When I look up at his face, I know he's not lying. Anyone who could do that to his nephew's face would have no problem hurting and killing someone he doesn't even know.

"What are we going to do?"

Jaxon winces from pain and gently touches my cheek. "We kill him before he kills us."

Horrified by the very thought of being responsible for someone's death, I shake my head, knowing he's right. "It's that simple?"

"It is."

We sit in silence for a long moment before he says, "I never wanted you to be touched by any of this, Tia. I swear I thought I could keep you safe. I was wrong. I thought we could be happy and not have to do the things I knew in the back of my mind would eventually become necessary."

"You told me once that loyalty was one of the most important things in your family. Are you really going to be able to kill your uncle?" I ask, not understanding any of this.

He smiles, and I swear even with a bruised face and swollen eye, he looks like an angel when he answers,

"I'll do what I have to so the woman I love is safe and we can have a life together. If killing Victor is that thing I have to do, then so be it. He brought this upon himself."

I know he's trying to make me feel better, but the way he talks about ending another person's life—his uncle's life—upsets me. I don't say anything, though, because he would probably think I'm being foolish. Someone tried to kill me and instead slit that poor woman's throat. Then they tried to kill us when I got shot. And they didn't give up, trying to run us off the road to try to kill us that way.

Maybe I am being silly. Why should I care about a person who wants me dead?

Jaxon touches my shoulder, tearing me out of my thoughts. "You got quiet there. Everything okay?"

I nod and try to smile, but it's a half-hearted attempt. "Yeah. Just tired, I guess."

Never a good liar, that's probably my worst effort yet. I don't want to talk about anyone else dying today. I'm just happy to be alive and have the man I adore here by my side again.

He slides his fingertip under my chin and gently turns my head so I have to face him. Still trying to hide how uncomfortable I am with him killing anyone, I push the corners of my mouth up toward my cheeks in what I hope is a believable smile.

"Talk to me, Tia. Tell me what's on your mind. I know you didn't get quiet because you're tired."

I push against his leg and roll my eyes. "I got shot, you know. It takes a lot out of you."

"Yeah, I know," he says in a low voice tinged with pain, like he can't handle hearing me talk about that topic.

"It's okay. The doctor Ryker had look at me said it went clear through, so it could have been much worse."

Pushing himself up against the pillows, he meets my gaze as he tries to smile. "I hate that my world has touched you like that. I know what it's like to be shot. I've had to dig bullets out of my body, and that's nothing I would ever wish on my worst enemy." He stops and chuckles. "Well, maybe on one or two of them. But the thought of you getting shot takes my breath away. It's every nightmare I've had come true."

"It's okay, Jaxon. I mean, I don't like getting shot, but I don't blame you."

He hangs his head and quietly says, "You should."

I hate seeing him like this. Jaxon is many things, and maybe most people wouldn't say a good man is one of them, but I see the goodness in him.

But I've always feared something like this happening because I know what's going on in his mind. He thinks he's to blame, but is he questioning if we should even be together because of all that's happened?

We sit in silence for a long time, but I have to ask

the question that fills my head. "Jaxon, do you regret ever being with me?"

He stares in horror at me for a few seconds as I anxiously await his answer. When he doesn't respond, I say, "I just want the truth. Honesty can't hurt us."

"Do you really think I could ever regret meeting you? Yes, I'm not thrilled with how it happened, but you've been in my system from the moment we met. When you left that house that day, I felt like someone had taken a part of me, like there was an empty space in the middle of my chest that made it hard to breathe, hard to even exist."

"But you broke up with me, and I know it was because you worried I might get hurt because of what you do for your family. If your uncle didn't want my father or me dead, would you have come back?"

I'm afraid I already know the answer.

Hurt fills his dark eyes as he says, "I missed you every day you weren't in my life. You have no idea how miserable I was without you, Tia."

"But would you have come back to me if I wasn't in danger?"

Jaxon hangs his head again, avoiding my gaze as he answers, "No. I would have stayed away so you were safe."

Even though I know he means well saying that, the truth hurts more than I expected. I turn away, not wanting him to see me cry. It's stupid, but I can't handle what he said.

"I need some fresh air," I say through gritted teeth as I struggle not to start bawling.

Jaxon tries to stop me, but I slip out of his hold and run out of the bedroom, slamming the door behind me. I have no idea where I am in this enormous house. It's not like I received the grand tour when I first arrived unconscious.

Stairs at the end of the hallway lead downstairs, so I hurry to them and rush down to the first floor. I just want to find a door to go outside and get that air I said I needed.

Kaia walks out of a room and sees me, and I sense she understands I need to get out right now. "Are you okay, Tia? Do you need anything?"

"I want to go outside. Can I do that?" I ask as I look around for any way to get out of this house.

"Sure." She takes me by the hand and carefully leads me to a door near the kitchen. "Do you want me to come with you? You don't look okay."

"No. Yes. I'm not sure. I just need to get some fresh air," I answer as I hurry toward that door that signals freedom, although I'm not sure what I want to be free from at the moment.

I barely get outside before the tears come fast and furious, and I can't stop them. I'm not even sure what I'm crying about. Getting shot? Thinking Jaxon was dead? Seeing him looking like someone took a baseball bat to his face? Or is it something small like that terrible, purple and black bruise on his abdomen I can't stop thinking about.

Maybe it's all of that, but mostly, I think I'm crying because if his uncle had never decided my father and then I needed to be dead, Jaxon would still just be a memory in my life. I wouldn't know there never was another woman. I wouldn't know how much he missed me.

I'd just be the person who missed him and wondered why he didn't love me enough to stay. But would that be any better than who I am now? Yes, I'd be safe, but would I be happier?

I walk around the estate until I find a bench near a garden where I can sit down. Part of me is so tired. That's probably because I was shot and then in a car accident. But another part of me wants to run far away from here. I want to run until no one can find me.

Even Jaxon.

Guilt fills me at that thought. I love him. I accepted what he does for a living because I couldn't imagine my life without him.

And then he left me, and for a year, I was miserable. I missed him more than I ever thought it was possible to miss anyone. Every night, I wished he'd come back to me and say he loved me like I loved him.

What is wrong with me now? I got all I wanted,

yet all I can think of is disappearing from this world of his.

I see Kaia walking toward me and wonder if maybe she can explain what I'm feeling. She seems to understand things, and right now, I need someone to tell me what the hell is wrong with me and what I should do because I'm so confused.

"Can I sit down with you? I don't want to intrude if you want to be alone," she says in that sweet way that I love right now.

Nodding, I shift over to the other side of the black metal bench. "Sure. If you have a minute, I'd like to ask you something."

She smiles like that makes her happy. "Absolutely!"

I try to gather my thoughts, but they're all over the place and not making much sense. I just need to say what's on my mind, and if it sounds crazy, I hope she'll be as understanding as I think she is.

Finally, I turn my body so I'm facing her and say, "I think there's something wrong with me, and I don't know what to do. I don't know if I can live in this world, Kaia."

She nods, and I think she knows exactly what I'm going through. Her gaze softens, and she touches my arm in that sympathetic way a mother does when one of her kids is upset or sad.

"Oh, honey, this world is hard on us. Don't blame yourself. You're thinking just what I've thought many times. I fell in love with Ryker, but I was in no way prepared for what it would be like to be married to him and completely immersed in this world he and his family live in."

I'm stunned by her words. "Really? You two seem so good together. I don't know how to explain it, but it's like you fit in with him fine. When I think of Jaxon and me, I stick out like a sore thumb, like I'm something wrong in his world."

"Why do you think that?"

Looking away, I finally say the thing I know is the problem. "He was talking about killing his uncle a few minutes ago, and it all sounded so casual and normal the way he was saying it."

I turn back to face her and continue. "I can't think of killing someone like that. I'm not sure I ever will be able to, and if I can't, then how can he and I be together? This is who he is, and I don't know if I can accept it now that I've seen it up close and personal."

She nods and gives me a tiny smile. "Oh, that. Yeah, I'm still not comfortable with that part of Ryker's world. He has to decide what he wants to do with his brother, and for what it's worth, he hasn't been able to bring himself to order the hit on Victor. I know it looks like these men don't view life like we do, but I think they simply see a different side to the situation."

"What side is that? Because all I'm seeing is someone dead."

"Think of it this way. Why would Jaxon want Victor killed? It's because of you. He knows those people who came after you two at the house and then rammed your car so you had that accident were sent by his uncle. To Jaxon, someone—and it doesn't matter if it's family or not—hurt you. For that, they have to pay."

I cover my face with my hands and wish she didn't say that. "I can't be responsible for someone's death, Kaia. It's just not something I can do."

"Oh, honey. It's not your fault if Victor dies. Trust me. If you knew what he's done throughout his life, you'd understand he's lucky he's made it this far."

My heart clenches at the way she says that, and I look at her when I ask, "But wouldn't someone be able to say that about Ryker or Jaxon? We wouldn't agree with that because we love them, but would they be wrong?"

My question seems to surprise her, and for a few moments, she doesn't say anything. Then, she takes my hand in hers and gives it a tiny squeeze like my mother always does when she knows I'm upset.

"Say that's true. Okay, maybe they aren't saints. Maybe they're the worst kind of sinner. Don't they deserve love like anyone else? I don't have to approve of everything my husband thinks or says or does in this world. I just have to believe he's a good man when it comes to me and our son."

The way she says that with such sincerity and

certainty impresses me. Has she thought the same kind of things I am now at some point in her relationship with Ryker?

"You don't sound like you have any doubts. I envy you. That's all I seem to be today."

A slow smile lights up her face. Patting my hand, she says, "My first husband was seen as a good man by nearly everyone who knew him. Upstanding. Handsome. Knew all the right things to say to make people think they should admire him. He gave me to Ryker to settle a gambling debt he'd run up. There are people in this world who to this day would say I should have gone back to him and be happy. Those people are wrong, but don't try to tell them that because they're sure Ryker is a bad man. I know in my heart that he's not the kind of man who would ever hand over his wife to anyone, especially someone who he believed might hurt or kill her. Society makes up these rules we think we're supposed to follow, and we do because it seems right. But what if it's wrong for someone?"

I'm stunned by her account of what her first husband did to her. What kind of person would do that to his wife? He sounds like a monster.

I've seen how Ryker treats Kaia in the short time I've been here. She's his queen, and he adores her. Yet, the rest of the world would think she would be better off with someone who didn't even care enough about her to put her above gambling debts?

Shaking my head, I try to find the words, but all I want to do is curse out that horrible first husband of hers. "That's terrible, Kaia. He wasn't a good person to do that to you. You deserved so much better than that."

"And I got it in my second husband. Ryker loves me and Maxim. Most importantly, he protects us, and even though most people wouldn't think that's important in this day and age, I can tell you from firsthand experience it is."

I think about what she's saying and can't deny being cherished and protected do mean something to me. I'd never thought about it that way because I was brought up in a middle class family where the most outrageous thing to happen was when someone in the neighborhood stole vegetables from my mother's summer garden one year.

Life isn't that simple anymore.

"You know, when Jaxon came to see me last week for the first time in a year, it was because he'd learned my father was in danger. I hadn't realized it until I was listening to you describe what Ryker is to you, but Jaxon wanted to protect me and the people I love. I think I was taking that for granted, but he didn't have to send my parents on a vacation to Italy to keep them away from Victor and his men."

"No, he didn't, but I can tell you that was the first thing he thought of when he heard Victor had put a target on your father's back. He wanted to protect you and make sure no one in your family was hurt. It was all he talked about. He didn't care about any of the details. He just jumped into action and knew he needed to see to it that you and your parents were safe. He may be a bad man in many ways to anyone who only looks at what he does for a living, but how terrible can he be if his first thought was protecting the woman he loves and the most important people in her life?"

I let out a heavy sigh as regret fills me. "I've been so stupid. How could I have not seen that?"

"Nobody is all good or all bad, Tia. My husband would be considered bad by many, but my first husband was considered quite a catch. Crazy, right? You have to decide what you can live with when it comes to the people you love. I can't tell you what to do, but I can say this. Jaxon would never let anyone hurt you if he could stop them. Victor's decided you and your father are marked for death. You did nothing to deserve that, and from what I understand, neither did your father. Jaxon wants nothing more than to protect you. You have to decide how good or bad that makes him."

When she finishes talking, she stands to leave. "I'll let you think about all of it. I know what you're going through. This isn't a life for everyone. You need to decide if you love him enough to accept what he is, good and bad."

"Thank you for telling me about what happened to

you. I didn't know what to do with all these feelings I'm having, but after listening to you, I know now. Thank you."

"I'll see you inside. When you're hungry, come down to the kitchen and I'll make sure you get a good meal now that you're up and around."

Alone, I feel ashamed at how parochial I was in my thinking about Jaxon. I was childish believing people are all good or all bad. That's just not how life is.

Now I just need to let Jaxon know I realize that.

CHAPTER FIFTEEN

axon

I STAND UNDER THE HOT WATER LETTING IT RUN down my body and questioning if I should have gone after Tia. She's too sweet for this world of mine. I've known that for a long time, even if I didn't want to admit it. Tia's a good girl, just like the day I met her. She doesn't know how to handle what I bring to her life.

With a sigh, I admit that truth, and I think that hurts more than any of the damage that shithead Dickie did to me. The swelling in my eye will go down. My ribs will feel better.

But Tia will never be able to see past what I do.

My brain kicks into overdrive as I begin to make plans to send her away. Fuck, I hate the idea of her gone from my side, but she deserves a chance to have the kind of life that doesn't involve people shooting her.

I need to find a way to contact my guy in Italy. She can go join her parents. Assuming Victor didn't get a hold of my phone, he doesn't know where her father is hiding. I know my uncle. If he had that information from my cell, he would have dangled it in front of me. Victor is nothing if not a gloater when he thinks he's got something on a person.

Defeated, I hang my head and let the hot water hit my back. It feels good, like a deep massage to make my muscles heal. I'd stay in this shower for the rest of time knowing what I have to do when I walk out into the bedroom, but that's not an option.

Tia must go. It was a mistake going back to her. I should have sent her on vacation with her parents in the first place. Then she wouldn't have gotten shot or sent careening off the road into a field and nearly killed.

I can get her to Italy tonight, and then I'll be able to focus on killing Victor. Unlike the woman I love, I have no problem with what I must do to him. I don't struggle with the ethics of killing, especially someone like him. He's hurt anyone who ever got close to him.

The reality is this is a kill or be killed situation.

Either we get Victor or he gets us. That's all there is to it.

And I have no intention of dying for that motherfucker to keep making the world miserable.

The shower begins to grow colder, so I turn off the water and dry off, all the while my gut twisting into a knot as I plot out how to send her away. The problem is I know I won't see her again after this.

How do you say goodbye to the only person you've ever truly loved?

I swipe my hand across the mirror covered in steam and take a look at my face. Fucking Dickie. I still look like a fucked up potato head with my eye nearly swollen shut and the bruises around my cheekbones and jaw. Motherfucker did a hell of a job on me. He better assume I'll do at least as much to him when I get the chance.

Who am I kidding? Fuck that beating him up shit. I'm just going to kill him.

For a moment, I search my expression to see any hint of regret for thinking that. Nothing. I'm a killer. This is who I am. I wanted to think I could be the kind of man who could have Tia too, but it seems those two don't work together.

But what if I walked away and only tried to be the man who loves her? It's not like Ryker, Cason, and Kane need me to kill Victor. I could leave with her tonight and run off to Italy to enjoy a wonderful vacation. We can take a ride in a gondola and see the

Colosseum. We can visit those places everyone raves about in Europe. Hell, we don't have to just visit Italy. I have enough money to take us to anywhere we want.

I catch a glimpse of my eyes and know that's all a pipe dream. A killer is who I am. It's what I need to be for my family. I can't turn my back on them at the very moment they need me most.

Even more, Victor stepped over the line when he went after Tia and her family. He knew how much I cared about her, and he still put a target on their backs. That kind of behavior can't go unchecked or unpunished.

Closing my eyes, I give myself a reprieve from that knowing look in them. Going on a wonderful vacation with the woman I love sounds great. Except I can't go. Not now. Maybe not ever.

Anyone who thinks men like me don't have regrets is fucking crazy. We have a lot of them. We just don't let anyone know.

I head out into the bedroom and feel relieved when I see Tia's not back yet. At least it gives me a minute or two to put off the inevitable.

On the bed are a pair of black pants and a blue dress shirt I left here a few months ago. Ryker better know how lucky he is to have a woman like Kaia by his side. How she tolerates having all of us around in her business here is beyond me. I would have told the entire bunch of us to get the hell out a long time ago.

As I gingerly slip my pants on over my very sore

legs, the bedroom door opens. I hold my breath as I wait to see who it is, and when I see Tia walk into the room, I wish I could say I was relieved.

I'm not. What I'm about to say to her is the hardest thing I've ever had to do in my life. Even harder than the words I said to her a year ago.

She gives me one of her sweet smiles before sitting on the edge of the bed. "You felt good enough to take a shower? That's good."

Nodding, I mumble, "Yeah."

"Are you angry with me because I needed to go outside and think for a little while?"

She really is far too nice for me. I need to keep reminding myself of that because if I don't, I'm never going to be able to get the words out I need to say.

I shake my head but turn my back to her to compose myself. I need to do this. Going back to her was a mistake she nearly paid for with her life. I can't risk that again.

"When I was outside, Kaia came to talk to me. She helped me see things I wasn't understanding, Jaxon."

"That's good."

She falls silent, which presents the perfect chance for me to tell her what I need to, but I miss my opportunity because I hesitate. I don't want to tell her goodbye. I love Tia. I would give my life for her, and the very thought of having to live without her forever hurts more than any bullet I've ever taken or any beating I've ever endured.

"Why won't you look at me, Jaxon?" she asks, her voice full of hurt.

I shake my head once more, but I don't answer her. I can't. I just need to say what's going to happen, and that's it. No emotion. No tears. Just say it and be done with it.

"So about everything. I'm going to make arrangements for you to join your parents in Italy. You'll be safe there. I can even add someone to the guy I have with your parents to make sure you're all safe."

The silence my words are met with is deafening. I can't even hear her breathing. It's like she's holding her breath.

I turn around, needing to see if she understands what I just said, and one look at her tells me she does. With tears in her eyes, she shakes her head but says nothing.

"It's for the best, Tia. I made a mistake coming back into your life. I didn't mean to make things worse, but now that I have, I need to fix things to make them right again."

She keeps shaking her head, but now the tears stream down over her cheeks. I have to stop myself from taking her into my arms because that won't help now. It will only make it harder for me to do what I need to, and she'll just get the wrong idea.

Finally, she wipes her eyes and stands up in front of me. I expect her to slap me across the face, which I deserve, but I'm stunned when she finally says something about my plans.

"No. I'm not going anywhere. And I can't believe you think you could just send me off like some unruly teenager to military school."

Okay. Damn. I didn't expect that response.

"Tia, it's for the best. You couldn't handle me talking about killing Victor, and I understand why. You're a nice person, and hearing someone talk about killing his uncle must have freaked you out. You don't belong in this world. You belong in a place where people are kind and nobody gets killed."

She steps closer to me and sets her hands on her hips. "I belong with you. That's all there is to it. Yes, I had a hard time before, but give me a little grace here. I'm new to all of this. You try being thrown into a world you know very little of and see how you handle it. I'm tougher than you think, Jaxon. I got shot and lived through it, for God's sake."

I can't help but smile at how sweet she is, even when she's trying to be a badass. "That's the damn reason I want you away from me and everything in my world. You got shot, Tia! Do you have any idea how bad I feel about that? I want to kill the guy who shot you right now even more than I want to kill Victor, and believe me, I want that bastard dead."

Shaking her head, she sighs, and I seize on that. "See? That right there. You can't handle this. I don't blame you. I blame myself. I was selfish and wanted you back, but I didn't think about how you'd do when push came to shove. Now I know."

"So now I can't sigh or show any emotion? That's complete and utter bullshit, Jaxon. So I don't like to hear you talk about killing people. So what? Does that make me unable to handle things? No, it doesn't. It just means that I don't like the thought of people dying, especially because of me. I'm not going anywhere, so get used to it."

I look into her blue eyes and wonder how I ever convinced this beautiful soul to love me. Whatever I did, I got damn fucking lucky she even gave a chance that first time I went to her apartment. Ninety-nine out of a hundred women would have told me to fuck all the way off out of their lives, and I would have deserved it.

"So now you're tough enough to handle this life? I don't know if you understand all that goes into being with me, Tia. I'm a bad man. A killer. Do you get that? Because that's what I am. Now's your last chance to get the hell away from me and meet some nice guy who can give you a new house, kids, and a minivan. If you don't go now, there's no way I'll ever let you go again."

She gives me one of her beautiful smiles and cradles my face in her tender hands. "You're not a bad man, Jaxon. You're a man whose job requires you to do bad things. I understand the difference now. And I don't want some guy who's going to hand me over to someone because he can't pick winners in a basketball game. I want you."

Confused, I shake my head as I try to figure out what she's talking about. "I think I missed part of our conversation because I have no idea what you mean. What guy? What basketball game?"

"Forget it. Just something I heard."

"Well, I don't know who you're talking to, but I'm not handing you over to anyone."

She stands on her toes and kisses me softly. "Good. Now that we got that settled, maybe we should do something about that eye of yours. I think it needs some ice to make the swelling go down."

"I thought it was looking better. I think it makes me look tougher, like a fighter. What do you think?"

Gently moving her hand along the side of my face, she touches just underneath my eye, making me wince. "I think some ice might help. Did I hurt you much?"

"No. The only thing that was hurting me while you were gone was thinking about how I had to send you away. Now that I know you're staying, I don't care how much pain my body is in."

Tia tenderly wraps her arms around me and rests her head on my chest. "Thank you for caring enough about me to protect my parents and me. I didn't realize how much that means to me until I was outside thinking about everything."

I rest my cheek against the top of her head and sigh at how good she feels in my arms again. "I'd give my life to make sure you're safe, Tia. Never doubt that."

Leaning back, she looks up at me and shakes her head. "Well, I don't want that. I want you around so when things calm down again, we can be happy." She wrinkles her nose and adds, "Things do calm down with all of you guys, don't they? It isn't always like this, is it?"

God, she can be so cute.

"Like any other job, it's long periods of practically nothing happening punctuated by bursts of way too much goddamned happening."

"Okay. I can handle that. I love you, Jaxon."

I kiss her and smile against her lips. "I love you, Tia. Never doubt that."

"I never do."

CHAPTER SIXTEEN

ia

"ARE YOU STILL REALLY SORE?" I ASK WITH AN ulterior motive about his answer.

Jaxon shrugs, unaware of my secret meaning. "I took a really hot shower, which felt incredible after my skin got used to the temperature, so I'm fine. Why?"

Tugging on his hand, I pull him toward the bed. "Well, I thought since we have this room all to ourselves and nobody's talking about anyone going anywhere anytime soon, we could take advantage of this bed conveniently being right here for us."

"Oh yeah?" he says in a teasing voice as he follows me across the room.

I nod my head and smile, wanting so much to show

him how I appreciate what he's done for my parents and me. Jaxon is my protector, just like Kaia made me see. I know all the bad parts of him, but for right now, I want to focus on the other parts that are nothing but pure good.

"I like where this is going. I do have to tell you I'm not sure I'm going to be able to be my usual self in bed, though. I'm feeling okay, but certain parts of my body aren't moving like they usually do."

Smiling, I look down his body and then back up at his beautifully bruised face. "I've got only one question. Is the part that makes my eyes roll back into my head working?"

He runs his tongue across his lower lip, leaving a glistening sheen on his mouth that makes me want to kiss him. "I think that part is fine. Thankfully, Dickie didn't do any damage to that part of me."

I sit down on the bed in front of him and slide my hands down the front of his pants. "Well, thank you, Dickie."

"Don't thank him for anything. The guy is a complete asshole. I'm not going to feel bad if I get a chance to give that fucker some payback."

"Okay, Dickie gets no credit, so no more talking about him. Now is just about Jaxon and Tia."

I lie back on the bed and look up into his dark eyes to see nothing but need in them. There are many things I adore about this man, but the way he looks when he wants me is just the sexiest thing I've ever seen.

"Do you remember that first time you came to my apartment?" I ask as the memory of that night fills my mind.

Jaxon nods and flashes me a sexy grin. "I do. I remember how much I had thought about you for days before too. You were like a drug and the antidote all in one, and I needed you more than I'd ever needed anything before in my life."

I watch him unbutton his pants and ease them down his legs, groaning when he has to bend over to kick them off his feet. As usual, he has nothing on underneath, and he's hard as a rock already.

Eyeing his hard cock, I look up at him as he looms over me. "I'm impressed. You were in a car accident and held hostage and beaten up, but still you're ready to go?"

He tilts his hips and drags his cock through my wet pussy. This time the noise that comes from him isn't about pain but pleasure.

"You were shot, in a car accident, and left for dead, but still you're ready to go. I'm impressed," he says with a chuckle before leaning down to kiss me hard.

"I have no excuse," I say with a giggle. "You have an effect on me."

"And you have an effect on me. But you always have."

Reaching down between us, I stroke the length of

him and watch that look of need come over him again. "Just watch my arm. It's a little sore."

"Then I think I should make the rest of you a little sore to match it."

I smile and he slowly thrusts into me, easing just the tip of his cock inside me. Lowering his mouth to mine, he kisses me long and deep and then slides into me until he hits that spot that never fails to make me moan.

"God, you feel so good, Tia," he says in a faraway voice.

Closing my eyes, I let the feeling of pure pleasure wash over me. "Fuck me. I need all of you, Jaxon."

He grunts near my ear, and it's like every part of his body now has a single goal. Make me come. I cling to his broad shoulders, loving how intense he is even after all he's endured today. He's wild and uninhibited, and I can't get enough of him.

I rock my hips back and forth, urging his cock to rub up against that perfect spot only he's ever reached. With each time he slides into me, my body craves that exquisite sensation.

When he looks down at me, all I can think of is how lucky I am to have him. Jaxon may be a bad man to the rest of the world, but he's the only man I want.

Sinking my teeth sink into his shoulder, I feel the first hint of my orgasm begin deep inside me. I wish our lovemaking could last so much longer, but something about being shot and thinking I'd lost Jaxon forever makes lasting much longer impossible.

He senses how excited I am and moans, "I've never felt you like this. What's different?"

In his ear, I whisper my answer. "I thought I'd lost you forever. Something about that changed me."

Jaxon begins to pump into me faster and harder, pulling my hair roughly. "When I thought you were dead, I didn't want to go on. It tore me up inside. The thought of never getting the chance to feel you like this again crushed me."

His dark eyes soften when I stare up into them, and I know just what he means. I slide my arms around his neck and kiss him like I've never kissed him before. Just knowing he's here with me after all that happened makes me happier than I ever thought possible.

I'm so close that I know it will only take a few more thrusts of his cock. Jaxon groans, and for a split second, I worry I've done something to aggravate his injuries, but then I feel him flood my body with all he has.

A few moments later, my orgasm tears through me, and I scratch my fingernails across his upper back as the most perfect feeling in the world takes over. I can't think of anything but how much I adore this man.

We still against one another, the two of us breathing hard as the remnants of our release linger and my thighs quiver. Jaxon slowly rolls off me and turns his head to smile at me.

"I think near-death experiences have an effect on us."

Nodding, I lean forward and kiss him softly on the lips. "Let's never have them again, okay?"

With an uncharacteristic sweetness in his eyes, Jaxon sighs and pulls me to him. As I rest my head on his chest, I hear him say, "I can live with that."

He may not be the typical knight in shining armor everyone wants in a man, but I'll take the bad because there's no much good in him too.

"I love you," I whisper against his bruised skin.

Jaxon kisses the top of my head and sighs again. "I love you too, Tia. I promise our life won't always be like this. Just give me a little time to get things straightened out, okay?"

He doesn't have to ask. I'd give him forever if I knew it would mean being with him.

CHAPTER SEVENTEEN

axon

RYKER IS ALONE IN HIS OFFICE WHEN I WALK IN, and I don't know why, but it's still strange to see him without that skull mask he wore for so long. I know why he stopped wearing it, but it's still odd.

He looks up from his desk and shakes his head at the sight of me. "Feeling any better? I mean, you look like shit warmed over, but I'm hoping you're feeling better."

I shrug as I sit down in the chair across the room from him. "Nothing I can't come back from. Where are Cason and Kane?"

"They went to get Lily and Lukas. I think they'd

be safer here, so Kane went with him since that kid's toys could fill a house by themselves. They took the goddamned Suburban because they need the space," he answers, laughing at the thought of Cason and Lily's kid and all his shit.

"That's good," I say as I look around Ryker's office and see some of Maxim's toys lying around. "They can be added to your kid's."

He sees the alphabet blocks on the couch and sighs. "I've told Kaia I just want this room to be kid-free. Just this room. I guess that's too much to ask."

I laugh out loud at his predicament, sure he's got much more pressing concerns to deal with than his son's toys getting into everything. "So this is what having kids does to a guy. I'll keep that in mind."

Ryker gets up and walks around his office collecting Maxim's toys before walking out of the room. No wonder we haven't moved on Victor yet. We're too busy playing romper room.

When he gets back, he sits down at his desk again and sighs. "Just wait until you have some. Then you'll know what it's like."

I don't bother telling him kids aren't in my plans any time soon. Maybe when I'm his age, but for now, Tia and I are far too busy enjoying one another to be focused on a baby.

Jesus, that sounds awful. A baby. Those things need to be fed and cleaned and diapered. And the burping. Then there's the spit up and the crying.

No, thanks.

In an effort to get him to focus on something that doesn't smell or shit its pants, I say, "I need to get a phone and contact my guy in Italy. I'm sure Tia's parents are fine, but I want to check, all the same."

Ryker's expression lights up. "Oh, about that. I have your phone right here. It was in the car. Victor's guys must not be very good at their jobs. I would have looked for your phone first thing after grabbing you."

Thrilled to see my phone, I take it from Ryker and sit back down to go through my texts. "Dickie wasn't exactly top level."

Just as I say that, my ribs on my right side send a message of their own as pain shoots through my torso. "Ugh, but he's got a hell of a right cross on him. I'm looking forward to the day I get to pay him back."

"Do you need to see the doctor?" Ryker asks, all concerned like I'm his kid too.

"No, I'm good, Dad," I joke, looking up from my phone to see a look of real worry on his face. "Seriously, I'm fine. Like I told Tia, I've dug bullets out of my own body before. This is nothing."

Smiling, he chuckles and asks, "How surprised were you when you walked in and saw her there?"

"I thought she was a goddamned delusion, man. Thanks for giving me a head's up."

"If I recall, I wasn't allowed to get two words in edgewise since you were busy telling me to basically go fuck myself yesterday. Am I remembering things incorrectly, or wasn't that you walking up my driveway telling me off?"

My guess is he thinks I'm going to apologize, but that's not happening. I stand by everything I said yesterday. In fact, that's one of the reasons I'm here this morning to talk to him.

"Yeah, and I think you need to hear more of that kind of thing because you haven't moved on Victor yet. What the hell is going on, Ryker? I know he's your brother. He's my uncle and Cason's fucking father. None of that changes the fact that the guy needs to be taken out. He nearly killed Tia and me. What the hell are you waiting for?"

I see by the angry expression that takes over his face that he's not happy I'm questioning him yet again on this issue, but I don't care. The time has fucking come to get rid of this Victor problem we're all dealing with once and for all. If Ryker can't or won't do it, then he better be prepared for someone else to step up to handle things.

"We've had this conversation, Jaxon."

Before he goes any further, I stand up and walk over to his desk. Leaning down, I get eye level with him. "Then why haven't you ordered the hit? What does he have to do, Ryker? Come in here and fuck around with you personally? That's not leadership. He has to fucking go, and it should have happened months ago."

Ryker stands from behind his desk, shaking his

head. "Do you want to lead this family? I'm still the head, so I decide what happens and when," he says in that low voice I know means he's on the verge of exploding.

Well, he fucking needs to.

"Nobody says they want to be the goddamned leader, dude. But if you're going to sit in the big chair, you have to make the big decisions, and those aren't happening. Victor took Lily hostage and threatened to not give her and Cason the baby back. Remember that? I thought you'd go after him then, but nothing happened. What is going on here that's holding up this show? Does he have to kill one of us before you'll accept your brother has to go? Because I'm not volunteering to be his next goddamned victim, Ryker."

He's practically seething by the time I'm done talking, but so be it. I don't know what's going on inside his head, but somebody has to get through to him that this inaction is putting us all in danger.

"You don't understand what goes into something like that, Jaxon. Until you do, sit down and shut the fuck up!" he barks.

That may have worked a few months ago, but after what Tia and I have been through, it's not going to play anymore. "No, and if you don't like what I'm saying, then ask any of the others around here. Ask Cason how he fucking feels about the specter of his father still looming over him. Ask Kane how he feels knowing Sophie is always in danger and he has to watch over her twenty-four seven because as a Varens, she's fair game to your dickhead brother. What the hell does he has to do to earn a trip straight to hell, man? Whatever it is, he's done it. It's time."

Leaning over his desk, he's right in my face but says nothing. I know what he's thinking. He isn't sure he wants to deck me, but he's sick and tired of me bringing up this same damn subject.

"It's complicated," he says through gritted teeth.

"No, it's not!" I bellow right in his face. "It's not fucking complicated, unless you're trying to make it complicated, which is seems like you are. He's got to go, Ryker! Now!"

I'm sure he's about to come over the desk at me at any moment, but the sound of someone clearing their throat gets our attention, and we both turn to look toward the door. Kaia looks at both of us like she's not sure if she wants to say what she came to the office to talk about or slap the hell out of the two of us.

"It's not a good time right now," Ryker says to his wife.

That gets him an eye roll. "I won't bother mentioning you seem to say that a lot lately. I just wanted to let you know that Tia and I are going to the store. Jeremy and Rico are coming with us. Maxim just went down for his nap, and the nanny is upstairs in the nursery with him. Do you want some of that mango juice you liked so much the last time I got it?"

The two of us just stare at her for a long moment

before Ryker turns to look at me and says, "I'll be back, but when I return, we won't be having any more of this conversation."

"Then you're going to have to block your ears because I'm still going to be talking about it."

Ryker doesn't respond to that and walks out of the office, leaving me alone for the moment. If he thinks I'm just going to let this issue of Victor needing to die go, he's got another thing coming.

I scroll through my messages and see my guy in Italy reported early this morning that Tia's parents are loving their vacation. They've traveled to Tuscany and are enjoying their time with wine tasting today.

As I'm texting him back, Tia pokes her head in and asks, "Do you want anything from the store? Kaia's got a list a mile long, but I know she wouldn't mind a few more items."

I wave her in and take her in my arms to kiss her. "Nothing is coming to mind, but if you see anything you think I'd like, feel free to grab it. More people are coming to stay, so she's probably shopping for them."

Tia taps the tip of my nose and kisses me. "She says Ryker loves this new mango juice she found. Would you like me to ask her to get extra so you can try it?"

The mere thought of that makes my stomach turn, so I shake my head. "No, thanks. I'm not a mango juice guy."

"You know, real men drink mango juice, Jaxon," she says, teasing me.

She really can be so cute. "Thanks for the vote of confidence that I'm a real man, but the answer is still no to the mango stuff. Now if you see some pineapple juice, I'll be on that in a hot minute."

Tia leans in and in a low voice says, "I thought we proved you were a real man last night. And this morning."

Pulling her to me, I hug her for being so sweet. "We did, and I plan to prove it again later."

After kissing me once more, she wriggles out of my hold and backs away toward the door. "So pineapple juice, right?"

I nod, loving how she's acting right now. "Yeah. And you know what I could really go for? Pizza bagels. I haven't had them in forever. Grab some of those."

"Pineapple juice and pizza bagels. Got it. Love you! See you in a little bit."

She's gone out the door before I can tell her I love her too. That's okay. I'll show her just how crazy I am about her later.

By the time Ryker walks back into the room fifteen minutes later, he's calmed down from earlier, but I'm still pretty hot about Victor not being dead yet. I don't understand what the hold up is. Yes, he's his brother, but even that old excuse has to give way at some point.

I busy myself with reading my messages, even

though I want to pick up where we left off. He seems focused on other things, though, and when Cason, Lily, Lukas, and Kane come into the house like a conquering horde, he turns his attention to them, probably to escape talking to me.

"Every Lego in the entire world is now here in this house," Kane says with more than a hint of disgust in his voice as he walks past the office.

Behind him, Cason laughs. "You just don't know how kids are these days, Kane. You'll see when you have some."

I swear that always comes off as sounding like a threat whenever he and Ryker say that to those of us who don't have kids yet. It's like they can't wait for us to be burdened by too many toys and stinky diapers.

When Kane pokes his head into the room, he looks at me and rolls his eyes. "I think we're going to need a bigger house."

I wave him in, eager to see if I can bring him over to my side on this Victor issue. "Hey, come here. I need to talk to you."

"What's up?"

"We need to get Ryker on board with this Victor business. The time has come, don't you think?"

Kane looks around, and I get the feeling he's worried about making sure Ryker isn't nearby before he gives me his answer. In a low voice, he says, "Yeah, but he's not ready yet, and pushing him isn't going to help."

"Well, something has to. Does he have to kill one of us before it's time?"

The stress of this whole situation is written all over Kane's face. "I know, but it's his brother. I need to go grab Sophie, but we'll talk more when I get back, okay?"

"Fine, but I'm done waiting. If this can't happen as a group, then I'll go do it myself."

Surprise flashes in Kane's eyes, like he can't believe that's where we're at already. He's always been more patient than I am, probably because he's not a Varens. I get it. He's loyal to Ryker above all else, but the time has come for loyalty to step aside in favor of action.

TWO HOURS LATER, EVERYONE IS IN THE HOUSE SAFE and sound with all their toys and everything else that they need. All except Kaia and Tia, but they're off getting enough mango juice for the entire family to enjoy.

Ryker, Kane, and Cason finally come into the office so we can have a meeting, and I'm ready to go. All he has to do is give the word and I'll be rolling over to Victor's estate, guns blazing.

The mood among the four of us is tense, no doubt because Ryker has either mentioned to them what happened before or Kane and Cason know what I'm going to say. Whichever it is, we're going to settle this issue today.

"So now that we're all settled and moved in, can we get to business?" I ask as Ryker sits down at his desk.

"We're not having that same conversation, Jaxon. I told you before."

I look around the room and see Kane eyeing up the door and Cason checking out the floor. Good to know they're willing to take a side here.

Well, if they aren't, maybe they just need a push.

"Have you asked Kane or Cason what they think?" I ask, and I swear Kane throws me a nasty look as soon as he hears his name come out of my mouth.

Neither of them say a word. Great. It looks like I'm flying solo on this one.

Then Kane surprises me by looking at Ryker and saying, "You may not like what Jaxon is saying, but I agree with him. Victor's time has come. He's only going to become more dangerous to all of us. I know he's your brother, but he can't be let to continue like he has. Jaxon had to send Tia's parents to Europe, for fuck's sake, and he and Tia were nearly killed."

I open my mouth to thank him for standing with me, but Ryker's already moved on to Cason for his opinion. "And you? Those two can say what they want, but it's your father and my brother we're talking about getting rid of here. What do you think?"

I'm more than ready to remind my cousin what his

father did when he kidnapped Lily and Lukas. I don't know how everyone seems to forget the shit Victor has pulled just in the past few years. It's like the whole family thing cancels out every terrible deed of his for the two of them.

Still looking down at the floor like he hopes to find the answer there, Cason sighs and simply shrugs. "Whatever you guys want to do is fine with me. The person I considered to be my father ceased to exist a long time ago."

Not exactly a ringing endorsement for taking action right now, but it's better than nothing.

Happy we might finally stop sitting on our hands when it comes to Victor, I stand up, ready to go. "Great! Then what's the plan?"

The other three men in the room don't move. Kane and Cason appear to be waiting for Ryker, and he's still sitting stone-faced behind his desk. It's enough to make me want to whip out my gun and start shooting up the goddamned place.

Just as I start to ask what the fuck is the hold up for the umpteenth time, Ryker's phone begins to ring. It's one of those old-fashioned black landlines you see in movies from before cell phones became a thing. It makes no sense that he keeps it, but then again, nothing he does makes sense to me lately.

As soon as he answers the call, the blood drains completely from his face. He quickly puts the call on speakerphone, and it doesn't take long to realize why he looks like he's going to be sick.

"So let me guess. Cason is there, of course. Jaxon? I'm guessing he hasn't found the time to kill his girlfriend's parents, which was the deal when I let him go the other day. And good old Kane, your trusty sidekick, right, Ryker? Did I get all the players correct?"

The sound of Victor's voice makes me want to fucking punch something, but Ryker seems distinctly upset. He doesn't answer his brother's question, so Victor continues to talk.

"Good to know. Well, as I said when you answered the phone, I've got some family visitors myself sitting right here in front of me. Want to talk to them?"

Ryker takes a deep breath in and lets it out slowly through his nose. "I've been respectful about who we are to one another up to this point, Victor. Whatever you're thinking about doing, you better reflect long and hard on it."

I don't understand why we care at all about whichever long lost cousins have dropped in at Victor's house, but then I hear a voice that makes it all clear. "Ryker, we're fine. He hasn't done anything bad. I don't think he will."

Kaia sounds terrified, but the way she said we're fine makes my heart skip a beat. Tia was with her when they went to the store.

"Your lady is being a bit optimistic, Ryker. I bet

you like that about her, though, don't you?" Victor asks with a sadistic laugh.

"Don't hurt her," Ryker says in a low voice that sounds like he wants to go through the phone and gut his brother like a fish.

Ignoring him, Victor says, "And she had a friend with her. Jaxon, how's that job you're supposed to do for me going? Now that I have Tia here with me, I'm thinking you'll get moving on it. Tick tock, kid. Which will it be? The parents or the girl?"

Rage explodes inside my brain, and I march over to where Ryker stands near his phone. "You hurt one hair on her head, and I swear I will make your death so fucking painful people like us will be writing textbooks for years to come talking about the most agonizing fucking way to kill someone."

The call falls silent for a second, and then I hear Tia's terrified voice. "Jaxon, I'm okay. Kaia promises me everything will be okay. I love you."

Laughing, Victor gets back on the phone and says, "You guys must have a thing for these sweet girls. I've never had one. What is the appeal? Maybe I should find out. Now before that, let me tell you why I called. No, it wasn't to let you know I'm going to have a good time with your ladies, although I am. It was to say I know what you're thinking of doing, brother, and I'd advise against it. I killed your snitch, but before I did, he was in enough pain to tell me what you're up to. So I thought I'd take out two insurance policies to ensure you don't do anything stupid. Ta-ta for now. I'll be in touch."

The line goes dead, and I swear I want to kill someone. Turning to look at Ryker, I ask, "So is it fucking time now? He's got Tia and Kaia. You know him. They aren't safe there. So what's it going to be?"

He sits down behind his desk without saying a word, but in his eyes I finally see the rage I've been waiting to see for months regarding Victor. Opening his desk drawer, he takes out his Glock and sets it on the top of the desk.

"It's time. My brother has gone too fucking far now, so we have to take care of him. I want to hear any ideas about how we're going to do this, but it has to happen today. We can't risk Kaia or Tia being hurt."

Thrilled he's finally ready to move on his brother, I push down my real fear that only Kaia will make it out alive. Victor wanted Tia dead before and did his damnedest to succeed at that. Now he's got her right there where he can do whatever he wants.

He better fucking pray he makes the right choice because if he doesn't, being gutted like a fucking fish is the very best he can hope for from me.

CHAPTER EIGHTEEN

EVERY PART OF ME QUAKES IN ABSOLUTE FEAR THAT at any moment I'm going to die. I've never felt this terrified in my entire life.

Jaxon's words about sending me away echo in my head, as do my claims that I'm tough enough to handle his life. What a fool I was to think that!

Kaia sits next to me tied to her chair like I am mine, our hands bound behind our backs and our ankles to the legs of our chairs. She seems so calm compared to me. I want to ask her how she's making it look like she's not scared to death, but Jaxon's uncle and some other guy about the size of a car are too close by for us to talk at all.

I knew the moment I heard Jaxon's voice that things were bad. Not that I didn't understand we were in deep trouble when those two guys grabbed us at the car after shooting both our bodyguards. But Jaxon only sounds like that when he's really upset or really scared.

He sounded like he was both.

Victor sits on a table with his legs hanging off like some elementary school bully watching us. I've been taking my cues from Kaia since she's playing it as cool as a cucumber. She never looks away when he stares at her, tilting her chin up ever so slightly in a defiant way that makes her look strong.

I haven't been able to master that look yet, so I'm simply trying not to burst into tears when he or that other guy even look at me for more than a moment. Unlike Kaia, I'm someone Victor wants to kill, and I can't seem to make myself forget that for even a few seconds.

"So you're the girl my son and then my nephew thought was worth the trouble?" he says as he looks over at me.

I have no idea how to answer that, so I try to smile, but it's a lukewarm grin, at best. I'm not sure what he expects me to say.

Uncertain if I should even respond, I try to appeal to something he may care about. His son.

"I knew Michael, yes. We worked at the summer camp together," I say, trying to sound confident and hopefully not giving away my true feelings on the bastard that was his kid.

Out of the corner of my eye, I see Kaia looking at me like I've done something wrong. I want to scream that I don't know how to react in this situation. I've never genuinely had a bad man take me hostage. Jaxon doesn't count because no matter what I've been assuming about him because of his job, he was never like this with me.

Victor hops down off the table and slowly walks toward where I'm tied to this chair. Stopping right in front of me, he seems to study me for a long time, like I'm an animal in the zoo that he doesn't understand.

I don't meet his gaze, instead fixing mine on the button on his suit coat. Much fatter than anyone else in the Varens family, his clothes seem to be ill-fitting, like they used to be fine on him before he gained a lot of weight but now they're barely holding all of him in. That button keeping his suit coat closed around his waist is doing what my mother calls "God's work" and at any moment might fly right off and hit me dead in the face.

"My boy seemed to have liked you at some point. Why?" he asks, and I think he truly wants an answer.

The only problem is I don't think I have one he'll like, especially since I'm sure I've just been insulted. Shaking my head, I try to play dumb. "I don't know. Maybe he liked blondes?"

Victor narrows his eyes and continues to stare at

me. "Hmmph. I've had blondes before. Nothing special. Pretty much like every other woman. No, I don't think that was it. Probably because you were a decent lay. That's all that kid ever thought of once he hit puberty. Yeah, that was it, I'm sure."

My instinct is to immediately tell him I'm in no way a good lay, just in case he's planning to try me out for himself, but I press my lips shut and keep my comment to myself. God, I want to be free from this place. Are Jaxon and Ryker coming to get us? Is that even possible?

I don't know how any of this works. I'm just a girl from a middle class family in North Carolina who happened to meet a guy and fall for him.

The thought of my parents immediately makes me wonder if they're still safe with that man Jaxon has taking them around Italy. Are they still there? Or did Victor find them too?

Squeezing my eyes closed, I try to will myself to not think about my father being murdered by one of Victor's hit men. I don't want to cry in front of him, but it's so hard to keep my emotions in check.

"She's just a girl, Victor. Leave her alone. She's never done anything to anyone."

My eyes fly open, and I turn to look at Kaia as she says that. Why is she speaking up? Doesn't she realize what this man is going to do to us if we piss him off?

He turns his attention to her, and for a moment, I'm relieved. Then he grabs her face and squeezes it between his fingers, making her cry out in pain, and I'm instantly back to being scared to death.

"Are you telling me what to do, Ryker's bitch? You should watch what you say. My brother may be nice to you, but now you're dealing with the real head of the Varens family, and I don't put up with mouthy bitches."

I watch as tears begin to roll down her cheeks and hate that she's suffering because of me. "Please don't hurt her. She didn't mean any harm. She's just worried about me because I'm so scared right now."

He looks over at me and once again doesn't seem to understand what he's looking at. I can't be that different from any other person he's ever seen, so I don't know why he stares at me so oddly.

"You know, I think I get why Michael and Jaxon liked you. It's that innocent girl thing. It's actually quite appealing."

I've never wished I appeared more worldly in my life than at this very moment. I want to look like a badass instead of some virginal thing he may want to try out. God, please don't let that happen.

Finally, he lets go of Kaia's face and pushes her head back hard. "You? I don't understand your appeal at all. My brother keeps you as his pet, and he ends up falling in love with you? I swear there's something wrong with that man. You use women like you. Use them and then throw them out when they don't please you anymore. You don't marry them and have a fucking kid with them."

As I listen to him detail what he thinks Kaia is useful for, I can't believe this man could be related to Jaxon or Ryker. How could they come from the same family yet he's so cruel?

Kaia continues to quietly sob as I try to figure out what's going to happen next. I don't want to let my mind go to a place that includes him raping one or both of us, but it's impossible not to think of that considering he sees us a disposable things worth nothing to him.

Finished with us for the time being, Victor walks back over to the table and eases himself back up onto it. His heavy breathing tells me he's not only fat but completely out of shape, so maybe if we could get loose, we might be able to run away.

Of course, the gun he keeps waving around is going to make our ability to run faster than his fat ass a moot point. Something about the way I say that in my head makes me smile. I sounded like Jaxon there for a brief moment. His cockiness might be rubbing off on me.

God, please give me the chance to see him again and tell him that.

"So, if I'm any judge of my brother and my nephew, they're going to come in here shooting the place to shit once they figure out how to breach the gates. Both of them aren't thinking clearly, though, which puts them at a disadvantage. You ladies are going to get to watch the whole thing on that monitor over there," Victor says with a smile as he points his gun toward the far wall.

"Why are you doing this?" I finally ask, unable to take the stress of being tied up and held by this madman anymore. "These are your family members. Why do you want to hurt them or hurt anyone they love?"

For a long moment, he just stares at me like before, and I'm immediately sure I've made a mistake by opening my mouth. I wait for him to walk over to me again and do something to me like he did to Kaia, but he doesn't move.

He just sits there with his legs swinging off the end of that table studying me. I'm like some butterfly under glass he can't seem to figure out.

Pointing his gun at me, he smiles and says, "Yes, they are my family. Not much good it's ever done me, but yes, we're family. My brother has worked against me ever since he was old enough to try to become our father's favorite. As for your boy Jaxon, he's my other brother's son but I treated him like he was my own. I gave that boy everything he could ever want."

Something in his voice sounds almost nostalgic, so I take a chance and say, "You sound like you cared about them at one point. Don't you think you could again? It's not like you can get a brother or nephew back once they're gone."

His eyes grow big, and I know in mere seconds that was a mistake. "I loved them! Ungrateful bastards! I loved them and made sure their lives were the best. They got everything they wanted from me, and now they plan on killing me! And why? Because I don't want to ruin the Varens name by being kindler and gentler. I'm a fucking businessman, for Christ's sake! Kindness can go fuck itself. I loan money, and I expect it paid back the way it's agreed upon. Those two think people should be given second chances. Fuck second chances! The world doesn't give second chances, so why should I? Ryker's gotten squeamish since he met this bitch and doesn't want to traffic women or drugs. What the fuck are we supposed to make money on then? What the fuck are we now if we aren't the family we've always been?"

He stops and jumps down off the table again, waving his gun even more erratically now. "I see what you're doing, you know. You think if you get me talking you'll distract me from what I plan to do. Well, it's not going to work, little girl."

"No, no. That's not it at all. I was just hoping you would reconsider killing people I care about."

Throwing his head back in laughter, he says, "Maybe I should just kill you two."

"No! That's not what I meant. I just meant that you care about Jaxon and Ryker. Maybe you don't have to kill them or us. Maybe we could all just keep living."

I hear myself and wish I sounded stronger and less naïve, but I'm desperately trying to keep this man from killing Kaia and me while hoping he won't be able to do anything to Jaxon and Ryker. I don't know what to do to convince this man not to hurt any of us.

"You are an interesting creature. I'll give you that. This one over here is the same old same old, but not you. I'm thinking I'm curious enough to know what makes you tick that I may let you live. You probably won't like what I'm going to do to you as you live, but you know you can't have everything in life."

Sensing I might have a chance to at least help Kaia, I seize on Victor's interest in me. "Then why not let Kaia go if you don't care about her?"

He leans down in front of me and gets in my face so I can't look away and says, "I didn't say I cared about you. Let's not get ahead of ourselves now."

Up close, he's absolutely horrific looking and smells like something deep fried. Unlike Jaxon and Ryker, he got none of his family's good looks. His eyes are too close together and a strange shade of brownish green that reminds me of something you'd find in a baby's diaper. Because he's overweight, his face is unnaturally full, as if he's hoarding food in his cheeks. Patches of hair dot his jawline making it look like he can't grow a beard too.

And as if all of that isn't bad enough, he smells like he's full of freshly deep-fried carnival food. I have to fight the urge to throw up with each second that passes and he's still right in my face.

"I know you don't care," I squeak out, "but if I'm the only one who interests you, send Kaia home. It might make your brother not want to come here and exact his revenge. That's one less person to deal with, and I know for sure that he never wanted to kill you."

Victor listens to me as I hurriedly say what I hope will convince him to free Kaia. I know that will likely mean I don't get out of here without something unspeakable happening to me, but at least Maxim will have his mother back.

Mostly, I'm hoping Jaxon will get here before anything really terrible happens with Victor.

Beside me, Kaia gasps in horror as I bargain for her release. "No, Tia! Don't give this man anything!"

In a flash, Victor slaps her hard across the face with the back of his hand. "Nobody asked your opinion, bitch!"

I watch in horror as she falls over in her chair, her head slamming off the floor. "Please, don't! I'll do anything. Just don't hurt her. Let her go. You don't like having her here. Let her go. I promise to do whatever you want. Please!"

My begging seems to appeal to him, and he nods like he's considering my suggestion. God, I hope he lets her go. That little boy with the big brown eyes who sat with me at breakfast this morning singing his ABCs deserves to grow up with his mother by his side.

Turning toward the other man standing on the side of the room, he says, "Take her out and leave her by the gate. My brother can pick her up when he gets here."

My hopes soar until the other man asks, "Can I do whatever I want with her first?"

Unable to keep my mouth shut, I cry out, "No! Don't hurt her!"

Victor's amused by my plea and shrugs as he laughs at me. "Make sure she doesn't have any marks on her if you do."

The giant man picks Kaia up chair and all and carries her out of the room unconscious. I can't stop myself from crying at the thought of what he's going to do to her before she's released. Oh, God. Please let her remain unconscious if it's something truly terrible. I don't want her to have to live with the memory of him raping her.

Alone with Victor, I hold my breath in anticipation of what he's going to do next. Whatever it is, at least Kaia isn't trapped in this room with him anymore.

I can only pray she'll be safely back with her husband and little boy soon.

CHAPTER NINETEEN

axon

OUR PLAN SET, THE FOUR OF US AND A HANDFUL OF Ryker's men prepare to move on Victor's house as soon as we can. The goal is to get there just after sunset, but I know that means Tia and Kaia will be alone with him for hours at that rate.

God help Victor if he hurts one hair on either of their innocent heads. Ryker's going to do what he needs to, but I plan to make his brother's passing from the Earth as painful as possible.

"Make sure you have enough ammo," Kane says as he sets a box of bullets on Ryker's desk. "We're going in hot, and I'm expecting some serious power to greet us."

Cason begins to say something about the best way to breach the estate when the guard at the front gate of Ryker's estate interrupts us on the intercom. "Is anyone there? I've got an emergency!"

Ryker runs over to the speaker on the wall. "What is it?"

"Mrs. Varens is out here, sir. She's in bad shape. Someone's roughed her up but good. I'm going to run her up there right now. She's going to need a doctor, though."

I hurry over to where Ryker stands and ask, "Is she alone? Isn't there anyone with her?"

"No. Just Mrs. Varens. I'm bringing her up now."

My heart sinks at hearing the news that Tia isn't with Kaia anymore. Victor's killed her. He followed through on his threat, and she's dead.

I stumble back into Ryker's desk, knocking over the box of bullets and sending them all over the place. Stunned for a moment, I don't know what to do. With Tia gone, I'm lost.

Then my anger wins out over my sadness, and all I can think about is smashing his head with a cinder block. That fucker took the only woman I've ever cared about, and now he's going to fucking suffer. If it's the last thing I do in this world, I'll see him beg for mercy as I pound his skull into mush.

The guard hurries in carrying Kaia in his arms,

and every one of us in the room stare in horror at how bad she looks. Blood seeps from cuts on her face, and where she isn't covered in blood, dark bruises have started to form. Her clothes are torn to shreds and barely covering her, and her legs have cuts and scrapes that make it look like she's been dragged behind a car.

When he sets her down on the leather couch, she lets out a moan that makes my chest ache. I can only imagine what Ryker's feeling at this moment seeing the woman he loves like this.

Her husband rushes over and falls to his knees next to her. "Kaia, I'm here. You're home, honey. You're safe."

She smiles and reaches out to touch his face. "Ryker? Is it really you?"

"Yeah, baby. I'm here. Nothing is going to hurt you now."

"Where's Jaxon?"

Everyone looks at me, so I walk over to stand behind Ryker. "I'm here."

I brace myself for what she's about to tell me. Tia's dead. I know it. She's dead, and for whatever reason, Victor didn't want to kill two women today.

"Jaxon, Tia made this happen. I'm alive and here because of her," Kaia says, barely getting the words out she's in so much pain. "She bargained with Victor to let me go. He wanted nothing to do with me, so she told him she'd stay and do whatever he wanted if he let me go. She saved me."

With a lump in my throat, I ask her the only question I care about now. "Is she still alive?"

I wait for the answer as my chest feels like someone's crushing it in a vice. All I want to hear is Tia's still alive. I can hope she's okay if I know he hasn't killed her.

Kaia smiles and slowly nods her head. "She was still alive when they took me out of there. She's so brave, Jaxon. She didn't fall to pieces or anything, and when she saw a chance to convince him to set me free, she took it. He likes her, so don't wait to go rescue her because I don't know how long she has before he does something to her."

She's still alive. That's all I needed to hear. Tia's alive, and she's waiting for me to come get her and take her away from that place.

"We need to go now!" I announce as I stuff my gun in my waistband. "She can't wait."

Cason and Kane look at me, but Ryker can't take his attention away from Kaia. I wait for him to say something, but he never turns around.

"Ryker? You coming?" Cason asks.

He lowers his head to kiss Kaia before standing up. "Yeah. It's time to take care of my brother."

"What about Kaia?" I ask, knowing how hard it is for him to leave her now. I don't think I'd be able to walk away from Tia if things were reversed.

Ryker smiles and looks down at his wife on the sofa. "She's the one who told me to go. Lily and

Sophie are here. They'll take care of her while we're gone."

"Go get Tia, Ryker," Kaia says in a soft voice. "I'm fine. I love you."

"I love you, and I swear I'm going to make this up to you, baby," he says, his voice full of regret.

She shakes her head and smiles up at him. "Just rescue her and give him what he has coming, Ryker. I'll be here when you get back."

I look over at Cason and Kane and see their concerned expressions as she says that. I know just what they're thinking. There's a chance we won't come back. Just like always in our world, at any moment it can be the last time we see the ones we love when a job like this comes around.

Ryker kisses her again, and I hear him whisper to her, "I'm so sorry, baby. This would have never happened if I didn't drag my feet. I swear I'm going to spend the rest of my life making it up to you."

"Just come back to me and Maxim."

When he finishes, he stands up and looks over at me. "Let's go. We need to get Tia back and kill that motherfucker."

It's taken far too long, but finally, Ryker sees what has to be done. Good. I just hope he understands I want the first shot at Victor. I know what he did to Kaia, but that son of a bitch has it coming in spades from me after all he's put Tia and me through.

CHAPTER TWENTY

Kaia

I WATCH RYKER AND THE REST OF THE MEN HEAD out to go to Victor's with a knot forming in the pit of my stomach. Dear God, I hope Tia is okay. I saw the way he looked at her like she was just what he'd like to enjoy, knowing it would hurt Jaxon more than any gunshot wound.

Even as I can picture the way he eyed her up like some kind of snack, I'm forced to acknowledge how much all of this hurts Ryker. That's his brother he has to kill today. He's avoided facing the truth about Victor for as long as possible, but that all changed when he took me.

I think that's what he wanted too. Victor wants

everything to come to a head because he thinks he's going to come out of this on top. I can only hope he's gravely disappointed.

Lily and Sophie talk in low tones nearby as I lie here on the sofa in Ryker's office, but I can hear what they're saying. Lily knows firsthand what Victor is like when he decides to take what's not his. I'll never forget how shaken she was after he kept her hostage and took away little Lukas. She wouldn't leave that child's side for months afterward, afraid if she did that Victor would find a way to steal him away.

"She's going to be okay," I say loud enough for them to hear.

They both turn to look at me and then come over to sit in the chairs nearby. Worry is etched into their faces, and even though they try to mask it with smiles, I know better.

"How are you feeling? Do you need anything right now?" Sophie asks.

I shake my head. "No. I guess I need to get up and take a bath, but that can wait. For now, I want to sit with you guys and…"

My sentence trails off, unfinished because I don't want to speak the words I was thinking. Hope our men are okay. Of course, they're okay. I know what they do for a living. They may have softened in their approach to the business in the past year or so, but being happy and having children has that effect on a man.

That won't matter when they meet up with Victor today. He stepped over the line when he took Tia and me. He broke an unspoken rule, and now he'll pay. He ceased to be Ryker's brother the moment he kidnapped me.

Lily reaches over and gently touches my hand resting on my stomach. "They're going to be fine. Cason may not have ever wanted this day to come, but he's told me over and over that when it did, he'd be ready. I know Ryker and Kane are too."

"And Jaxon has been chomping at the bit to take care of Victor for ages," Sophie adds. "I know we don't want to see them have to do this, but he's out of control. Kane told me he's known for a while something would bring this whole situation to a head. I just don't think he expected it to be Victor taking you and Tia. That was ballsy even for him."

The only Varens by birth among us, Sophie has always seemed stronger than Lily and me. More than once, she's mentioned to me in quiet moments that she's never feared her uncle being taken out. He's never actually done anything to her, but she grew up hearing what kind of man he was from her father, a man who refuses to even be in the same room with Victor.

He's become an outlaw to his own kin. It didn't have to be like this, but the time has come. He must die. Today.

"Jaxon was right the whole time," I say in a low voice.

"Do you think she's still alive?" Lily whispers, like she doesn't want to say those words too loud in case Tia's gone already.

I look at her and Sophie and nod. "She was so strong back there. I don't know where she found the courage to say some of the stuff she was saying to Victor. Tia's got no experience with anything like this, but she made sure I got out of there. I'll never be able to repay her for that."

"Strong is good," Sophie says. "Strong means she can take a lot. I know what she's going through. I had to be strong with those bastards who took me. I had Kane, though. She's all on her own with my uncle, and I wouldn't wish that on my worst enemy."

Lily nods, and she should know. Victor held her hostage to get to his son, and she's told me she wasn't sure she'd make it out alive.

"I hope he didn't do anything to her. He can be so cruel. I used to worry that Cason would turn out like his father. I told him that, and he swore he would never want to be like that man. I should have known he wouldn't become like Victor. After all, he's never forgiven him for killing his mother. That kind of thing leaves scars that never truly heal."

We sit in silence for a long time as the possibilities of what could be happening to Tia float through my mind. I push each one out, but then it's replaced with something even more horrible.

Finally, to make myself feel better, I say out loud, "I know Tia is going to come out of this okay. The guys are going to take care of things, and she'll be back here safe and sound tonight. She may not have been brought up to be tough enough, but she's got it in her. I saw it firsthand. She's going to be fine."

Lily and Sophie nod their agreement, and all I can hope is that I'm right.

God, let her be okay. Bring her back to us so we can take care of her.

CHAPTER TWENTY-ONE

ia

FOR THE PAST TWO HOURS, VICTOR HAS PACED BACK and forth in front of me as I sit here tied to this chair wishing I could do something to hurt him. Then again, even if I wasn't bound at my wrists and ankles, what could I truly do? He has a gun. I have nothing. I'd be no match for him.

All he seems interested in at the moment is asking the giant man guarding me if he hears noises. I don't know what he thinks is happening, but I haven't heard anything.

Even admitting that makes my heart sink. Where is Jaxon? Why hasn't he come to find me yet?

Then a truly terrible thought enters my head. Did

Victor already have him killed? Is that why he hasn't come for me?

Almost as if he can read my thoughts, Victor stops in front of me and grins. "Strange that your boyfriend hasn't come riding in like the knight in shining armor yet, isn't it? I thought he'd be here by now."

Relieved to hear him talk about Jaxon as if he's still alive, I say, "He's coming. You know that."

I don't know where my bravery is coming from. Before tonight, if anyone had asked me how I'd handle myself in a situation like this, I would have freely admitted I'd cry, pass out, and probably be dead in a matter of minutes.

But something in the way Victor listened to me when I said he should let Kaia go has emboldened me. I'm not that scared girl his dead son trapped in that big house years ago because he wanted to terrify me. I don't know how it happened, but I'm strong now.

However, no matter how strong I am, I won't be able to fend off Victor's advances if he decides it's time to rape me. I know he has no love for women of any kind, but I seem to occupy some strange place in his mind that so far has helped me stay alive and untouched.

I don't know how much longer either of those states will continue, though.

Victor nods his head and sighs. "I know. I taught him how to work in this business. Did you know that?"

"I do. He's told me what you did for him," I say, hoping my gut feeling is right and this man has some familial feelings that still exist for his nephew.

And by extension, me.

"He did?" my captor asks, clearly surprised.

Nodding, I choose my words carefully, aiming to keep his focus on his love for his family. "Of course, he did. He said he knew nothing when he came to work for you. He told me you taught him everything."

"And he stabbed me in the back the first chance he got," he says in a voice full of rage before he starts pacing again.

"He didn't mean to," I say, my voice verging on pleading. "It's just that he wanted different things."

I don't finish that sentence the way I want to by adding when he met me, but that's the reason why Jaxon started working with Ryker instead of Victor. He didn't want to be involved in trafficking women and drugs. He wasn't trying to be a good man, but he didn't want to be that man anymore.

The problem is I don't think Victor understands that.

"My brother thinks this family can live on that bullshit he's got going on," Victor says, stopping briefly in front of the man on the side of the room who nods his agreement. "He wanted to stay dealing with fucking gamblers, but I told him that's not something men like us do anymore. Fuck, it's legal to gamble on fucking phones nowadays. What the hell would make anyone want to bother with bookies then? He talks about hacking and other bullshit, but that's not what people like us do. Why can't he understand that?"

I don't say anything, but he proceeds to answer his own question, spinning around to face me with a look of rage in his eyes. "It's because he fucking settled down! I'll never understand how that bitch changed him. He used to wear that mask and act like a Varens should. Now he spends his time playing fucking pattycake and other domesticated nonsense. And I'm the bad guy here?"

My plan isn't working. I keep making him angry when I'm trying to get him to see he doesn't have to hurt me because he's upset with his family.

When he stops in front of me again, I consider simply asking him to let me go. He did it with Kaia, so he might do it for me too.

But then he reaches out to touch my cheek, and I see in his eyes something that makes my blood run cold. "You really are very pretty, and it's definitely that innocent girl thing. I should have known Jaxon would fall for the likes of you. Do you know he one time set free one of the girls I was selling? She started talking to him, and lo and behold, a few days later, he asked me if he could have her. I figured he meant to fuck around with, so I said yes, and the son of a bitch let her go. It took me a fucking week to track her down. Then when he found out I sold her anyway, you would have sworn I shot someone he loved. She was a whore, for God's sake! But she had big blue eyes I swear you could get lost in. Sort of like yours."

Hearing Jaxon cared enough about someone to want to help them reinforces my belief that he's not the kind of man he claims he is. Yes, he does bad things, but a truly bad man wouldn't try to help a girl to safety.

Victor slides his hand down over my jaw to encircle my neck. Smiling, he says, "You're going to be fun to play with, little Tia."

I can't stop my fear from producing a noise that sounds like a moan, and he mistakes it for my wanting him. He couldn't be more wrong. Everything about him sickens me, from the way he looks to the way he smells to the kind of man he is.

I'd tell him that too if I didn't think it would get me shot in the head. I don't know how to play this because I had hoped he'd never get the chance to do anything to me, but Jaxon hasn't arrived to save me yet, so I'm on my own.

And I've never been more terrified in my life.

He moves his hand down to my shirt and in one pull rips it down the middle, exposing my bra underneath. Ogling me like I'm some piece of meat, he licks his lips, smacking them as if he can't wait to taste me.

"Please don't do this," I say in a shaky voice I wish sounded tougher at this moment.

Looking up from my breasts, he smirks. "Don't

worry. My second wife was like you. She got used to it. You will too."

I tightly squeeze my eyes shut, in part to hold back the tears and in part so I don't have to see what he's doing. Holding my breath to avoid smelling him as he leans in and fondles my breast through my bra, I silently pray to God to let me pass out.

Oh, God. I can't handle this! Please, somehow don't let him go any further.

His fingers press into my tender flesh, hurting me. "Nice tits. I like that."

My emotions swirl inside me, threatening to make me break down into a sobbing mess, but I find the ability to control myself and take a deep breath, filling my lungs with that disgusting fried food smell that emanates off him.

I can do this. Whatever he does to me, I can handle. It's not sex. It's not sexy. What he's doing is nothing short of rape, and while it's more horrible than anything I've ever experienced, I can make it through this.

I have to.

Moaning as he rips my bra off my body, Victor says in a low voice, "Oh, I'm going to enjoy this. And the fact that your boyfriend will always know I had you is like a cherry on top of the cake."

All that bravado I filled my head with a few moments ago practically disappears when he starts to move his hands down to my jeans. I steel myself for what's about to happen next, swearing to myself I won't fall apart.

Even though that's all I feel like I can do right now.

"So the tits are nice, but they're just the appetizer. Now let's see the main course," he says with a laugh.

Everything about him is repellent, so all my body does is recoil at the mere thought that in a moment he's going to be stuffing his hands in my pants. He breathes heavily, hopefully because he's a fat fuck who's completely out of shape and not because he's excited, but I can't tell. Not that it matters. I can't stop what's about to happen next.

Every muscle in my body stiffens in pure terror as he trails his stubby fingers down over my ribs on his way to that main course he's so interested in. I'm powerless to stop him from doing anything physically, but I won't let him get to me.

The first touch of his hand inside my pants does me in, and I can't stop myself from crying. It's involuntary, and I wish I could make it stop, but I can't. Here I sit in this horrible room with that enormous man in the corner probably watching Victor do this to me, and all I can do is squeeze my eyes shut as tightly as possible even as my tears stream down my face.

I'm strong. I can handle this. This isn't sex. This is just about his power over me. Nothing else. I'm still alive. That's what matters. Not what he's about to do to me.

I hear him grunt like a pig as he tries in vain to jam his fingers inside me. My pants are too tight and don't allow him the access he needs. I've never been more thankful to be wearing a pair of jeans.

As I await that horrible moment when he rips them off and does what he wants, I hear a noise like what I think a gunshot might sound like. Has Jaxon come for me?

Suddenly, Victor stops pawing me, and after a few seconds I open my eyes to see he's walked over to talk to the other man. I try to see the monitors he's watching, but they're too far away and my eyes are still full of tears.

Then I hear him say the words I've been praying for.

"They're here! Time to make some magic, Dickie."

I breathe a sigh of relief, but I don't want to rejoice too soon. Even if Victor doesn't want to rape me anymore, that doesn't mean Jaxon and the rest of the men are safe.

Just as I'm sure Victor is preoccupied, I see him turn toward me holding a knife and wearing a smile that terrifies me. "Time for those jeans to come off, little Tia."

All I can do is scream in the hopes that Jaxon can hear me and burst into the room before Victor gets what he wants.

CHAPTER TWENTY-TWO

axon

WE WALK INTO VICTOR'S HOUSE, AND THE FIRST thing I hear is a scream I know is Tia, making my heart skip a beat as we all march past the dead bodies of Victor's men. I expected far more guarding the estate and the house, but they seem to have all vanished when he needs them most.

Not surprising. The guy is a complete dick to work for, so why would anyone lay down their life for him?

"She sounds like she's in that room downstairs," Cason says, pointing the way.

Someone rounds the corner from a hallway and

takes aim at us, but Ryker quickly blows the guy away. Two more follow that guy and meet with the same fate, dropping where they stop.

I've never seen Ryker like this. He's like a killing machine, and I'm here for it one hundred percent. It's about fucking time.

"Feel like getting a little target practice in?" Kane asks as we step over their dead bodies and try to avoid the blood and brains that sprayed everywhere behind them.

Ryker turns to look at me and shrugs. "Just doing what I came here to do. Stay sharp. Victor may have told his men to stay close to him to lure us into a false sense of security and think this is going to be a cakewalk."

Just as he gets that last word out of his mouth, two more poke their heads out from behind a wall near the kitchen. Itching to kill someone, I lift my gun and pop the one on the right in the middle of his forehead. He drops like a fifty pound bag of flour, leaving only his buddy next to him.

"I got him!" Cason calls out, and a second later, he pumps two into the guy, sending him falling to the floor like his friend did a few moments ago.

Just beyond them is the door that leads to the basement. Beyond that door, it's a narrow set of stairs I'd rather not spend much time in. It'll be like shooting fish in a barrel if there's more than one guy waiting for us.

We stand there for only a few seconds before Tia screams again, and even though I know I should wait for what our plan is, I can't. I charge through that fucking door with my gun ready to kill anyone who gets in my way of saving her.

I hear Ryker say something about having my back as I take the stairs two at a time. The first of Victor's minions waiting for us downstairs begins shooting before I can even see him, so I spray the fucking area in front of me, hoping I catch him at least once.

Behind me, Cason and Kane call out when they see one and take their shots, helping me get down to the bottom of the stairs. Once I turn the corner, there's another one waiting for me, though, and he's had fair warning we're coming.

"You're not getting through here," he says with a shitload of bravado, if not a whole lot of brains.

I raise my hand to shoot him, but he gets off a round before I do, catching me on the arm. The spike of pain sends me stumbling back into the wall. The guy says something cocky about enjoying this, yet a second later the only thing he's enjoying is a shot to his face courtesy of Ryker.

"I've heard enough talking out of these assholes today," he says when he stops to help me.

Waving him off, I push the pain away and shake my head. "I'm good. We need to get to Tia."

"You sure?" he asks, looking down at my arm and the blood starting to soak my shirt.

"I'm fucking fine. Let's go!"

As we pass the one who shot me, I kick him in the side for fucking hitting me. "Asshole. In your next life, work for a better boss."

I still haven't seen Dickie, but I can only hope he's with Victor. With any luck, I can get a two-for-one deal and kill them both.

The house falls silent, which tells us all of Victor's outside men are taken care of. Now we just have to deal with anyone protecting him inside that room we think he's in.

We all stop outside the door for a few seconds as Ryker silently motions that he wants to lead the way. I think about arguing with him since I'd love to be the one who takes out Victor, but I understand why he wants to be the person who gives his brother what he's got coming to him.

I have no idea how many men he has inside with him. It could be one, or it could be a dozen. I don't care. The time has come to take care of fucking business.

The next minute goes by in a blur. Ryker throws the door open and is instantly hit by a shot from Dickie. Happy to take care of that asshole, I aim for his fucking knee and shoot. He collapses to the ground screaming in agony. I watch with a certain sense of glee as he writhes in pain, but I'll get back to him later.

Cason disarms him as I begin to look for Tia, but

Dickie's the only person in this room. "Where the fuck is she?" I bark at him.

He laughs even as blood pours out of his leg. "She's gone. He took her, and trust me, he's already had her, Jaxon. She screamed, but she was no match for him."

I can't see straight I'm so enraged. I rush over to him and kick him in the head, sending a bunch of his teeth flying out of his mouth. That's not enough for me, though. I want to beat the hell out of this fuck not only for what he did to me but for gloating about what Victor did to Tia.

There's no time to waste on all of that, though, so I smile down at him and take aim, making sure to do a little gloating of my own. "Time to meet your maker, motherfucker. Your boss will be along in a minute. Fuck you, asshole!"

He opens his mouth to say something, but the bullet drives into his forehead, slicing through skin, bone, and brains like a hot knife through butter. It wasn't exactly the ending I had planned for him, but it will have to do.

Kane and Cason are already on the other side of the room heading out the door that leads to the estate grounds, so I hurry to catch up with them, wondering where Ryker has gone. "We're missing someone. Where the hell did Ryker disappear to?"

For a second, I wonder if he's changed his mind

about taking care of Victor. That's fine with me. I'm happy to step up and send that son of a bitch straight to hell.

Cason answers me as we run out into the estate just as the sun sets. "He ran after my father."

Fears about what Victor's done with Tia fill my head as I look around in the dim light for any sign of them. If she becomes a problem for him and slows him down, he'll get rid of her. She's a means to an end, but if he thinks she's not going to help him, I know him. He'll put a bullet into her head and run off.

We have to find the two of them before she becomes a liability for him.

In the distance, I hear a gunshot, and I freeze. It feels like forever until the next sound hits my ears, but when I hear Tia scream my name, I take off running across the lawn toward where I think she and Ryker must be with Victor. Behind me, Cason and Kane yell they're going to cover me, but I don't care about my safety.

All I care about is getting to Tia.

I run as fast as I can, my eyes scanning the grounds around me, but I don't see them. I need her to let me know where they are, so I call out, "Tia!"

For a long moment, I don't hear a thing, but then she screams, "Jaxon! I'm here!"

My heart soars, even as I can't deny I'm afraid of what I'm going to find when I reach her. I come around a row of hedges, and there on the ground I see

Victor with Ryker standing over him. Tia lies a few feet away, and all I can see when my gaze lands on her is her shirt is ripped in half.

I run over to her and drop to my knees beside her on the grass. "I'm here, Tia. I'm here. You don't have to be afraid anymore."

She sobs my name and something else I can't understand, but it doesn't matter. She's alive and safe with me. That's all I care about. Ryker can take care of Victor. I have what's most important to me now.

Taking her in my arms, I cradle her against me as she continues to cry. "I thought you weren't going to get here in time," she says against my chest.

"I'm sorry I was late. Forgive me."

Tia gently pushes me away and smiles up at me. "For your birthday, I'm going to buy you a watch. Then you'll be on time."

I shake my head at how she could be making jokes right now. "Okay. I guess I can start wearing a watch again."

Her smile makes me think she's going to be okay, after all. I know it's going to take a long time for her to get over what's happened today, but I'll be there with her every day and every step of the way.

Then she sees the blood on my arm, and her eyes grow wide. "Oh my God! You're hurt!"

Smiling, I shrug, not feeling even a twinge of pain from where that asshole of Victor's shot me. "It doesn't matter. It doesn't hurt. All that matters is you're okay."

Exhausted from all she's been through, she doesn't say another word. Tia just rests her head against me, but that's fine. I can be strong for both of us.

That's what the man who loves her is supposed to do.

CHAPTER TWENTY-THREE

yker

I STARE DOWN AT MY OLDER BROTHER LYING ON THE grass at my feet and think about how when I was a boy I idolized Victor. He was so confident compared to me. Our father always thought he'd succeed him because only Victor was strong like him. I wanted to be like this person, and now all I want to do is kill him.

"Just fucking do it, Ryker. Have the balls after all to do what's necessary. Then you can go back to your life of wedded bliss. You'll be haunted by my death at your hands, though. I let you live when I didn't have to. Remember that."

Victor has always known what to say to get into my head. It's why I've hesitated all these months to do what was needed when it came to him. I knew what he was up to and how he was a risk to all the people I cared about, but I couldn't forget the time he had me in a very similar situation as right now with his gun pointed at my head and let me go.

That was a long time ago, though. I was a different person. Maybe he was too. I don't know. So much has changed in the time since that day. I swore I'd never let myself be put in that position again and walked away from the way he wanted to run our family.

And now, we've come full circle. Now, he's the one who needs me to show him mercy.

But I can't do that. He's done things that are unforgivable, even in our world. He hurt the woman I love. His actions have hurt the Varens name. He's out of control and has been for far too long.

So now I have to do the worst thing a brother can do.

"I never wanted things to come to this," I say, staring down into eyes that remind me so much of mine.

I'm shocked at how he looks these days. In my mind, he's always been bigger than life, but now he's just a bloated old man. Then I look again and see how much he resembles our father at the end of his life. Overweight and worn down by years of corruption and living a life full of hurting others, including his family, our father wore the ugliness of his soul on the outside of his body.

"Since you've sat on your hands forever, I knew you didn't want to do this. You still don't. I would have killed you the second I saw you if you took something I cared about. You've always been like this, though. Our father knew that. It's why he put me in charge of the business."

I smile at his sad attempt to stoke my rage. "He chose you because you were older and just like him. It was that simple."

"He knew I could make the Varens name even greater than he made it. He was right," my brother smugly declares.

I think I always knew this moment would have to happen. If I was younger and didn't have Kaia and Maxim when he went off the rails, I may have been as eager as Jaxon to snuff out Victor's life. I'm older now, though. I've got other priorities than the business, so maybe my brother is right. Maybe he was better at leading the family.

It doesn't change what I must do.

"Jaxon wanted to be the one to kill you for what you did to him and Tia. Your son wouldn't mind being the one to send you to hell either. What does that tell you, Victor?"

He doesn't even bother to think about my question before he practically spits the answer out. "It tells me they're fucking pathetic like you. Once I'm gone, what are you going to blame everything on? Once I'm not around, who is Jaxon or Cason going to say is making their lives terrible? You need me."

I look up and see Cason watching his father taunt me. He frowns and shakes his head before looking away.

"See? Even your kid doesn't think you're worth it. What you never understood was we were all family. You didn't have to try to get rid of us. All you had to do was remember we're your blood."

Victor looks back at Cason and laughs. "He was always too much like his mother anyway."

Even seconds before he's going to die, he still doesn't have a kind word for his son. What a legacy to leave this world with.

My finger twitches on the gun as my hand begins to shake. "Tell Dad I was the one who did it."

A moment later, the bullet explodes out of my gun, killing my older brother with one shot to the head.

The world feels like it stops for a long time, as if it ceases turning as I stand here staring down at my brother dead by my own hand. Some part of me always knew this day would come. I didn't want to admit that for a long time, but once I did, I still couldn't bring myself to imagine it would be because of me that Victor would come to this end.

I hear my father's words echo in my brain. "Ryker, to be a leader, you must do what's necessary. That isn't always the right thing or the thing that makes you feel good, but it's what must be done."

He used to say things like that to me all the time, and I never understood why since Victor was always going to be the head of the family. That's the way my father wanted it, so what would I need to know about being a leader?

So many times, I asked myself that question since I could never ask him that, but the answer eluded me. For many years, I assumed my father said that to me as a way of justifying Victor's actions that I'd have to deal with in years to come.

Now I know that wasn't true. My father likely knew at some point I would want to lead the Varens family, and to do that, I would have to eliminate the one person who would stand in my way.

My brother Victor.

I watch the blood flow from his body, the last sign of his life, and wonder if I should feel anything after all he did in this world. If so, then there must be something wrong with me because I feel empty. That's it. Empty. Not sad. Not unhappy.

Just empty, like a void.

As I think about that, I can't help but smile. My father would love seeing me like this. He always believed I was too feeling. I let my emotions control me, and for him, that was the worst thing a son of his could do. That's why he believed Victor was a natural leader, and I wasn't.

So now that I feel nothing for my own brother's death, I'm sure my father would approve. I don't know if I do, though. For as much as Victor did to me and the people I love, and as much as his actions weren't in line with my beliefs regarding how business should be conducted, he was my blood.

And now he's nothing.

"We need to get going," Cason says as he stops next to me on his way to the car.

I turn to look at him and ask, "Are you okay?"

Far more like me than his father, Cason answers in a distinctly Victor-like way. With a shrug, he says, "Sure. Whatever that person was, he hasn't been my father since he killed my mother. If anything, he had this end coming a long time ago. You just gave him more time. More than he deserved."

I glance down at Victor again as Cason walks away without another word and can't help but feel like that's my brother's legacy. His own son can't even be bothered to shed a tear at his passing. That says a lot about a man.

If I do nothing else in this world, I can only hope when it's my time, Maxim will care that I'm gone. To be someone who no one misses when you leave this world is a crime no man should commit.

Kane walks up to where I still stand and nods before looking at me. "You know you had to do it, right?"

"Doesn't make it any easier."

"Fair enough," he says before sighing. "Would it

help for me to remind you that he would have happily sent you out of this world without a second thought?"

"No. He never gave a damn that I was his brother. That's where we were different. I actually cared."

"Then let me remind you he took your wife," Kane says flatly.

I shake my head and chuckle at his attempt to make me feel okay with what I've done. "It's all right. I know I had to do this. It's not like I'm bawling my eyes out over it."

My dear friend slaps me on the back and begins to walk away. "Good. He was never worth anyone's tears."

Jaxon and Tia walk the other way so she doesn't have to see Victor's dead body. I don't know what my brother did to her, but she's going to need a lot of support for a long time to come. Thankfully, she's got Jaxon.

"Come on, Ryker," Kane says in a low voice. "It's time to go."

I look around my brother's estate and nod before turning to walk to the car. Tomorrow, the news will report the head of the Varens crime family was murdered tonight. The police will congratulate themselves on a win. One more villain gone from this earth. The people he hurt will rejoice at his death.

And no one will care the day after tomorrow. Not a life well-lived at all.

CHAPTER TWENTY-FOUR

axon

Since we returned to Ryker's, Tia has been uncharacteristically quiet. I need to hear her say something, but she simply walked directly to the bedroom and into the bathroom to take a shower. Now she's sitting on the bed staring down at her crossed legs after getting dressed.

"Are you hungry?" I ask, unsure what to do to get her to talk.

She shakes her head but doesn't look up at me.

"Do you feel okay?"

I wait for a few moments before she nods but still says nothing.

Concerned about what's happening, I sit down next to her and wrap my arm around her shoulders. She doesn't flinch, which I was worried about, but she simply sits as still as a statue. It's as if all her emotions have left with her words.

"Tia, please talk to me."

Seconds tick by without her saying a word. I lean my head on her shoulder and sigh, not knowing how to reach her. I know what happened at Victor's is affecting her. That's why I want her to talk to me.

Actually, my need to hear her say something is far more selfish. What if she isn't talking because she's decided she can't handle living in my world after all she's endured? What if she has no words for me now because there's nothing more to say?

"Tell me what you're thinking."

I watch her draw her eyebrows in like she's on the verge of crying, but no tears appear. She remains silent, either unwilling to tell me what's on her mind or unable to.

Climbing off the bed, I walk around in front of her and try to meet her gaze, but she won't look up at me. I sit down and take her hands in mine, and I can't help but notice how small they are next to my hands.

"Please, Tia. Say something. Tell me you're okay. Tell me what happened. Tell me to fuck off and leave you alone. Just say something. I can't handle this silence."

Her little finger on her right hand twitches against

my palm, and then she falls still again. I don't know what to do. She's lost, and I can't seem to reach her.

After a long while, I gently set her hands on her legs and stand from the bed. "I'm going to get you something to eat. You must be hungry."

I have no idea if she wants to eat or not. I just need to do something or I'm going to lose my mind tonight.

As I walk across the room toward the door, I hear her finally say something in a tiny voice. "How do you do it?"

I don't need to ask do what. I know. How do I handle seeing people hurt or killed and still go on?

Slowly, I walk back to sit next to her. "The first time I saw someone die, I felt like I was going to puke. I couldn't show that, though, because Victor would have ridden my ass about it, so I pretended I didn't give a damn about watching someone bleed to death in front of me. Then, the first chance I got, I went to the bathroom and threw up until I cried. He told me I'd get used to it, but I'm not sure that ever happens."

She shakes her head and then looks over at me with tears filling her eyes. "I don't know how I'm going to ever sleep again, Jaxon. He did horrible things to me, but I can't handle knowing I'm to blame for his death."

Cradling her beautiful face, I kiss her cheek damp from tears. "Tia, you aren't the reason Victor Varens is dead. I need you to understand that."

"If I wasn't there with him, you all wouldn't have come to kill him."

I press my forehead to hers and close my eyes. "He died because of the things he did for his entire life. Tonight was just the final time he'll ever hurt someone like you."

She's silent again for so long that I have to open my eyes. I see her staring at me and lean away.

"That's the truth. I need you to believe that."

Wiping her eyes, she asks, "What about you? What's going to happen if someone decides you've done things that make you deserve to die?"

I take a deep breath as I try to think of an answer for her. So much of my world involves gray areas we all prefer not to dwell on. We chose this life and know what that means.

But Tia never chose this. She simply chose me, and this life came along with me.

"That's always a risk for someone who does what I do. I've learned to accept that. I do things I have to live with for the rest of my days. Some are hard to justify. What happened tonight isn't. Even if Victor had never done a bad thing in his entire life, just taking you and Kaia was enough to warrant what he got."

I can't bring myself to utter a single word about what he did to her down in that basement because it makes me want to kill him all over again. He hurt the most important person in my life. If I could have been the one to aim that gun and send that bullet through his fucking brains, I would have done it with glee.

That was Ryker's job, though.

"I don't know if I can do this, Jaxon. I love you. I need you to know that. But I don't know if I can live in your world," Tia says with so much sadness in her voice that my heart clenches.

I hate seeing her like this. I love her with everything I have, but if being with me is going to make her so unhappy, how can I do that to her?

She's too sweet for me. She always has been. That I've had as much time with her as I have is a miracle.

Taking her hand, I press it over my heart and look into her eyes when I say the hardest words I'll ever speak. "There's never been anyone but you. There never will be. But I can't make you stay where you can't. That's not fair to you."

Her eyes open wide, and she asks in a shaky voice, "What are you saying?"

I swallow hard and say the very thing I've feared the entire time I've been with Tia. "I'm saying you deserve to be happy. If that's not with me because of what I do, then I'll have to accept that. I love you, Tia. You're everything to me. It's because of that I have to let you go if you can't live in my world."

"Let me go? I don't understand, Jaxon. Why are you saying this?"

"Because I'm a killer, baby. It's who I am. Now

you've seen what I do, and my biggest fear has been realized because you can't live with it."

Tears roll down her cheeks as she shakes her head. "No! I don't want to lose you again."

"We are who we are, Tia. That's always been the truth from the moment you walked into that coffee shop and met me for the first time. I should have never done Michael that favor. If I hadn't, you'd be happily living your life and never have to go through what happened tonight."

"And I wouldn't have you!"

I hang my head and say the words she has to hear. "A killer who held you hostage for his cousin, kidnapped you, got you shot and in a car crash, and ..."

Those final words don't come out because I just can't say them out loud. I know Victor raped her. I can't speak those exact words, though.

"Would you have killed him because he touched me?"

Without a hint of hesitation, I answer, "Yes. I won't apologize for that."

"I don't want to lose you, Jaxon. I don't know what to do. I can't live with the life you lead, but I don't want to live without you. What do I do?"

She's slipping away from me right before my eyes, and I can't do a thing to stop her because she's right. My world is no place for her. She'll never be truly happy if she stays with me now, and I can't be the reason she's unhappy for the rest of her life.

"I can give you anything you want in this world, Tia. I have enough money to afford anything your heart desires. Homes, cars, clothing, jewelry, yachts, vacations, and everything else under the sun. I'd happily do it because you mean the world to me, and seeing you smile is worth every dime I have. But what you want I can't buy."

Tia throws her arms around me and begins to cry against my shoulder. "I don't want things. I want you. Why can't I have you?"

I hold her against me, loving how she feels in my arms and knowing this may be the last time I get to experience this. "You shouldn't want me. You should want someone who doesn't live like I do."

She leans back and looks at me, sniffling as her tears keep coming. "I don't want anyone else. I want you. Tell me how that can happen."

Tia knows as well as I do that's not possible with who we are right now. Something has to change, and I can't expect that from her.

I slip my arms from around her and ease myself off the bed. "I'll be back. I want to get you something to eat."

She hangs her head and won't look at me as I walk out of the room.

. . .

Ryker's sitting in his office when I walk in, and I have to say I'm surprised to see him at work already. Taking a seat in one of the chairs in front of his desk, I shake my head.

"You should be with your wife and boy now, dude."

He smiles like he knows and doesn't need to hear that from me. "They're both sleeping. I wanted to come down here for some peace and quiet since I figured everyone else would be busy tonight."

I imagine he's right. Kane and Sophie are in their room, and Cason and Lily are in their room, along with Lukas in his room.

"Why are you down here?" he asks, leaning back in his chair.

As hard as what I'm about to say is, it's time. "Tia's got to go home. I'd like your car to get going in the next few hours."

"Does this mean what I think it means?"

Nodding, I try to smile, but it's impossible now. "Yeah."

"Are you sure about this? As the head of the family, you know I'm supposed to ask you that, right?" he says with a chuckle.

"I know. Yeah, this is for the best. She doesn't belong in our world. It's not fair to expect her to find a way to deal with the life I lead."

"If your father could see you now, Jaxon."

What would he say, I silently wonder. I don't

know. Maybe he'd think I'm crazy for giving up what I've cared about for so long. Maybe he'd understand.

All I know is I can live with this, even if it means losing something important to me because it's the right thing to do.

I stand up and laugh at that thought. "Do you know I just thought to myself that I have to do this because it's the right thing to do?"

"Look at you. All grown up now. Don't be a stranger, okay? Just because you aren't working for me anymore doesn't mean you can't come visit every once in a while."

He extends his hand and I shake it. "Got it. Come back every so often, or I'm going to get a surprise visit from every Varens in this house."

"You have to make sure to come back for Cason and Lily's baby's arrival. Or at least the christening. It wouldn't be a party without you, Jaxon."

"Damn right. Tell everyone I said I'll see them later, okay?"

"Will do," he says with a smile. "Take the SUV. I have a feeling you'll need it."

As I walk toward the door to go back upstairs to Tia, I roll my eyes. "Let's not rush things, okay. We're young. We've got lots of time."

"Cason and Lily are younger, and they're going on their second one," he says behind me. "You guys need to catch up."

For a moment, I get serious with him. "We have

some stuff to work through on that front, thanks to your brother."

Ryker frowns, letting out a heavy sigh. "I'm sorry about that. Is she going to be okay?"

"I have a feeling when I tell her my news it'll be a step in the right direction. I'll be there for her."

"You're a good man, Jaxon. Don't forget that."

I shake my head at that idea. "That's a first. I don't think anyone would have ever thought to say that about me."

"Well, you are. Go live your life and be happy. Just don't forget us, okay?"

Stopping in the doorway, I nod. "Thanks for everything, Ryker. And thanks for not being like your brother."

If Ryker was like him, he'd have no choice but to kill me to ensure I never leave the family.

But things are different now. Victor was the old way. Trafficking women, drugs, and guns. Killing anyone who crosses you. He never left the past, but Ryker knows the Varens family can't live back there.

That's why I know they'll be fine without me. The new way doesn't need enforcers much. Between the online gaming company Victor owns and the hackers he's got working for him now, that world Victor and his kind have been clinging to will finally fade away for Ryker, Cason, and Kane.

I can only hope they'll be as happy as Tia and I will be.

. . .

SHE'S SITTING ON THE BED WHERE I LEFT HER WHEN I return to our room. I start packing her things up, and then grab my things to stuff into the bag.

Confused, she walks over and looks at my bad packing before looking up at me. "What's going on?"

"Time for us to go," I say brusquely, trying to keep the smile off my face.

"But I told you I don't want to go. Not without you."

Finally, I can't hold back my happiness and smile at her. "Then I guess I'll have to go with you."

"What? What do you mean? Like driving me to my house and then leaving?" she asks, barely holding back the tears.

"No. I mean we're going home, Tia. You and me. A fresh start for us."

Her eyes grow big, and she throws her arms around me as the tears start again. "Oh, Jaxon! Really? You're going to leave all of these behind? For me?"

"I can't think of a better reason. Now let's get going. We've got a long drive ahead of us."

She kisses me and sighs. "I don't know what to say."

"Say you like the idea of living with me since I never asked and sort of sprung this on you."

Tia gives me a big, beautiful smile. "I love the idea

of us living together. Are you sure about this? I don't want to be the reason you leave your life behind."

I cradle her face and press my forehead to hers. "You're the only reason I'd do anything, baby. I love you."

"And I love you, Jaxon. Thank you for understanding."

Holding her to me, I close my eyes and smile. "I hear that's what good men do."

"You are a good man, baby," she whispers in my ear. "I suspect you always have been in all the ways that matter."

That's debatable, but if being with Tia means I need to be that kind of man, then that's what I'll be. She deserves that from the man who loves her.

Keep reading to find out more about Abbi's dark romances!

ALSO BY ABBI COOK

Captive Heart (standalone prequel to the Captive Hearts series)

Behind The Mask (Captive Hearts #1)

Beneath The Surface (Captive Hearts #2)

Beyond The Lies (Captive Hearts #3)

Before The Fall (Captive Hearts #4)

Captive Hearts: A Dark Romance Mafia Collection

Rule (Villains Club #1)

Take (Villains Club #2)

Burn (Villains Club #3)

Play (Villains Club #4)

Bang (Villains Club #5)

Villains Club Collection

Savage Mine (A Born Villains Prequel)

Savage Heart (Born Villains #1)

Ruthless Touch (Born Villains #2)

Vicious Rule (Born Villains #3)

And be sure to sign up for Abbi's newsletter if you haven't already! You don't want to miss a delicious word and all the great things with each release, and subscribers receive a FREE book just for signing up!

ABOUT THE AUTHOR

Romance you love with the darkness you crave

Abbi Cook grew up wondering if she was different because she always wanted to know more about the villain than the hero in the stories she read. When she got older, she found there were others in the world like her and devoured their writing, loving every dark word. She's written her own tales for years, but in 2019 she decided it was time to take the next step and publish them. She's never looked back since that day.

Readers can find her at her website at abbicook.com, on FB and IG, and through email at abbicookauthor@gmail.com